No Rest for the Wicked
The Heart of a Hero Series

Cora Lee

ISBN 9781944477035

More Than Words Press
PO Box 480 042
New Haven, MI 48048

Cover by Elaina Lee, For the Muse Design.

Editing by Jude Simms.

To the everyday superheroes who fight to make this
world a better place.
Thank you.

WHAT IF YOUR favorite superheroes had Regency-era doppelgangers? And what if a group of them were recruited by the Duke of Wellington to gather intelligence for him during the Napoleonic Wars while they protected their own parts of the realm?

You'd get The Heart of a Hero series.

And this is how it begins.

He will soon find that there is no rest for the wicked, no place on earth wherein the criminal can hide his devoted head.

—Joseph Moser, Esq.
Zemira; or, The Fisherman of Dehli, An Oriental Tale,
1807

Chapter One

Dublin, July 1808

Joanna Pearson stood in front of the door deep within the part of Dublin known as The Liberties, trying to decide what to say to the occupant of the room beyond it and to quell the strange feeling in her stomach. Her previous missions had been straightforward enough: locate the subject, relay the invitation from her employer, and make arrangements for the subject to travel securely on the appointed day.

But none of the other subjects had been her estranged husband.

It had been five years since she'd last laid eyes on him, sleeping peacefully in their bed. Light from the rising sun had illuminated his dark hair and long lashes, giving him a faintly angelic appearance that contrasted starkly with the scars on his body. Her courage had nearly failed her then, and she'd had to stop herself from lying back down beside him. But a spy didn't get to choose her missions, and Joanna had slipped quietly out of the door without looking back.

If only this door was as easy to negotiate as that one had been.

She could hear his voice inside, ringing with the refined English accent of the educated. There came several muffled responses, a flurry of movement, then the door flew open and a knot of children rushed out.

Joanna jumped out of the way, listening to them chatter among themselves as they made their way down the stairs. She peered around the doorframe and, seeing no further traffic, quietly entered the room.

Michael Devlin was bending over a small table paging through tattered books, his back to the door. But before she'd completed her first step inside the room he straightened.

"Joanna?"

He spoke without turning around—he'd always been good at detecting her presence—so she addressed the back of his white linen shirt in the soft Dublin brogue she'd been practicing. "Michael. It's been a long time."

He thumbed the topmost book closed. "If you've come looking for your husband, I'm afraid he might need some convincing to speak with you."

"I expect he would—and I owe him that much, at the very least. But it isn't my husband I need today."

"Oh?"

She swung the door closed and moved further into the room. "I need to speak with the Demon of Dublin's Hell."

He turned sharply at that, his eyes locking onto hers. "Why?"

"I have a message for him."

"What message?"

Knowing he wouldn't come to her, she crossed the remainder of the small chamber before handing him a sealed letter. "Your presence is requested. Or rather, the Demon's is."

"By whom?"

"See for yourself."

He took the letter and broke the wax seal, his brown eyes slowly scanning the page. "Sir Arthur Wellesley?"

Joanna nodded, catching the familiar scent of Michael's shaving soap. "He's a lieutenant general now, readying a large force to sail to the Continent."

"How do I know this is really for me? It isn't addressed to anyone, and the details are rather vague. It says only to meet him in Cork."

"A security measure," Joanna replied. "If the letter missed its intended recipient, no one would know who the recipient was—he's doing business with plenty of people in Cork before he sets sail."

"And you?" Michael lifted his gaze to hers, his lips pressed together for a moment. "Are you a security measure as well?"

She tilted her head slightly, giving his question some thought. "I suppose I am. Not only to deliver the letter—"

"—but to ensure my cooperation," Michael finished, his boyhood brogue creeping in. That brogue only slipped out when he was tired or doing battle with his emotions, and Joanna was willing to bet this time it was the latter. "He thinks if he sends my wife with his instructions, I'll be more likely to follow them."

"I was sent to the others, too," she told him, keeping her voice as matter-of-fact as possible. "But Sir Arthur did think you might be...more reluctant than the rest."

"You said it's the Demon of Dublin's Hell that Wellesley wants. Does he know that *I'm* the Demon?"

"He does."

Michael held the letter tightly with both hands and read it again. "What does he want with me?"

"A meeting."

"Do you know what the meeting is about?"

"Not all of the details, but I know that it isn't sanctioned by the Army. In fact, no one in a military or governmental position is officially aware of Sir Arthur's request. This is strictly his own personal affair."

"And?"

Joanna clasped her hands loosely behind her back. "And you are to arrive no later than one week from today."

"A week?" Michael shot back, shaking the letter at her. "He wants me to just abandon my city and those who depend on me so I can run off to Cork...for reasons he won't deign to share with me?"

Joanna didn't even flinch at his display of temper. Michael was certainly capable of violence, but he'd always had a strict code about who was on the receiving end of it. And while a runaway wife suddenly returned would merit serious verbal censure, she knew he would never physically harm her.

"Arrangements have been made to take care of all your responsibilities while you're away," she explained in an even voice. "*All* of your responsibilities. And while I can't tell you much about Sir Arthur's plans in Cork, I can tell you exactly what will happen in Dublin while you're with him."

He sucked in a breath and held it for a moment, letting it out slowly before speaking again. "*If* I agree to go."

"I know that this is a lot to take in. I also know that a dearth of information makes you uncomfortable, and I've provided very little."

Michael threw her a glance that was all downturned mouth and glowering brows, but he remained silent. She watched his chest rise as he took in an even deeper breath than before, watched his shoulders ease a fraction as he exhaled. He repeated the exercise once more, then dipped his chin in a curt nod.

"You are right, of course. The more information I have, the more comfortable I feel."

The more in control he felt, though he'd never admit it. And with the paucity of information she'd supplied thus far, he would not be feeling very in control just now.

"Is there somewhere we can sit and talk like civilized people? I'll tell you as much as I am able, and you may ask all the questions I know are buzzing about in your head."

His whole body visibly relaxed at her pronouncement. "There's a small sitting area in my bedchamber. We can talk quietly there without fear of being overheard."

The second of his two rooms was even smaller than the first, with only enough space for a bed, a washstand, a diminutive writing table, and a single chair. Joanna occupied the chair, her features as placid and unrevealing as the plain black dress she wore. That unnerved Michael more than her abrupt appearance at his door—he had always been able to read her, even when she was immersed in a mission.

But not this time.

He settled himself at the foot of his bed, trying to decide which questions to begin with.

"You said arrangements had been made to cover my absence." He pressed his palms against the mattress. "Tell me everything you know about them."

A tendril of red hair had come loose from Joanna's practical coif, and she tucked it behind her ear—a gesture he'd made for her so many times before he could still feel the softness of her curls against his skin.

"An associate of mine is making her way to Dublin as we speak. She can take up the Demon's post and look after The Liberties in your absence."

"Who is she?"

"Cara Campbell. She once occupied a position similar to the Demon's in Belfast."

"She once occupied that position? But not any longer?"

Joanna shook her head. "She does some lower profile work now. But she is more than qualified to take your place as protector for a time."

"She gave it up?" His fingers curled into the rough blanket that served as a coverlet. "She just walked away from the people who looked to her for safety? How do you know she won't do the exact same thing to Dublin?"

Joanna folded her hands together in her lap and leaned forward. "Because her guardianship of Dublin is for a finite period of time. As soon as you return, she can resume her own activities—or seclusion—as she desires."

"I want to speak with her before I make any decisions."

"As you wish. I will make the introduction when she arrives."

He gave her a brief, uncertain nod, wondering how he'd won that point so easily. One of the ways they'd shown affection for each other had involved debates and arguments, all of which had been long and drawn out.

"What about my clients?"

"You have only one, which you should be able to hand off to a colleague before your departure," Joanna answered without hesitation. He felt his eyes widen and the corners of her mouth turned up in a small smile. "Not really surprising—Catholics might be allowed to practice law now, but that doesn't mean people will hire them."

"I do well enough," he replied, trying to keep the defensiveness out of his voice.

She gestured to the room at large. "Well enough to keep yourself in all this lavishness."

Michael's fingers slid forward to grip the footboard. "I am where I need to be."

She was quiet for a moment before replying, "I know you are. No neighborhood gains the moniker 'Hell' because all is safe and well."

His fingers loosened on the footboard. "But Wellesley wants me for something else, and I still haven't heard what it is."

"He is assembling a group of individuals to form an intelligence ring of sorts," she explained. "Something he learned in India—spies and information gatherers are priceless commodities."

"No doubt they are, but I'm no spy. Espionage requires a finesse that I do not possess." He let his eyes take in her image, the picture of an ordinary working class Irish widow right down to the worn but serviceable shoes she wore. Yet she was none of those things. "Subtlety and cunning were always your strong suit."

Her smile grew. "They still are. But you won't need them. The idea is to gather everyone together in Cork, lay out your responsibilities should you choose to become involved, then send everyone back whence they came. Once you're home again, you will pass along to Sir Arthur whatever you discover, but won't be assigned any missions on the group's behalf."

"I see." Michael would be free to resume both aspects of his life in The Liberties as though nothing had changed, then. And Wellesley had built up a reputation as a fine commanding officer with a good head for strategy during his time in India. He had also served a brief stint as Chief Secretary for Ireland, supporting a more moderate enforcement of the Penal Laws, to the relief of Catholics all over the island. Did that cleverness and open mind earn Sir Arthur the right to Michael's presence in Cork? Would there be some benefit to The Liberties in the longer term if Michael established connections with others like himself? Perhaps. He had to admit the idea was intriguing.

Whether or not he would actually go along with this secret society of Wellesley's remained to be seen.

Joanna settled back in her chair, her smile taking on a slightly smug quality. Michael guessed that she had watched his thought process play out on his face, knowing the conclusion he came to at the same moment he did.

"I will go, but only if certain conditions are met."

"All right then, name your price."

"In addition to meeting your Miss Campbell, someone must take over the children's reading lessons while I'm away."

Her brows rose a fraction. "Is that what they were doing here when I arrived?"

Good. There was at least one thing she didn't know about him. He leaned back a little, shifting his palms back to the mattress. "They come when their families can spare them and I help them learn what they can. None of them will ever study at Trinity, but a good apprenticeship isn't out of the question."

"Then I will find someone to continue working with them."

"I also want you to explain what happened between us. I awoke one morning to a vague note saying you needed to take care of something and that you'd be back in a month or two. It didn't say I'd have to wait five years, wondering the whole time who you might be with, or if you were even still alive."

Joanna was silent for long moment, her eyes focused on a point just beyond his shoulder. "After Sir Arthur's gathering."

Michael had expected that. She'd always insisted on reaching her objective before indulging in personal business. "Fine. When my dealings with him are concluded, I will hear your account."

"Then I accept your conditions. All of them."

"Good," he said, pushing himself off the bed and stretching to his full height. "Assuming I approve of your Miss Campbell, I will go to Cork and see what Sir Arthur has planned. Though I reserve the right to revoke my consent at any time."

"Of course. You aren't my prisoner." She stood beside him, the top of her head barely reaching his chin. "But first we must find you some new clothes."

Chapter Two

"THIS IS EVERYTHING?"

Joanna stood beside Michael, staring at the traveling case that contained his everyday clothes. She'd rifled through it when he produced it from beneath his bed, but had frowned and stepped back after only a moment.

"This is everything," he confirmed, wondering why his clothing was important. What did she want with a few shirts, several pairs of trousers, stockings, and smallclothes?

She swung her gaze to his. "You're a solicitor—surely you don't see clients in this attire?"

"Oh, of course not. I have finer clothes for clients." He bent and pulled another case from under his bed, flicking open the latch and throwing back the lid for her inspection.

"Better," she said, running her hand over a red silk waistcoat. Was she remembering that he'd worn it at their wedding?

He did, every time he put it on.

"This will do nicely."

"For what?"

She lingered a moment longer over the waistcoat before answering. "For traveling. It is much easier to travel as a person of some fortune. One gets better service and more privacy that way, and we'll need the privacy."

"We're traveling together?" He balled his hands into fists at his sides. Naturally there was more to the story than she'd told him. There always was. "And why will we need privacy?"

"There are still things to discuss about your stay in Cork, and we won't want those conversations to be overheard." She returned her attention to his clothing and began spreading things out on the bed.

"You will be playing the grand lady, then. But if I act as your footman or groom, any time we spend alone together will arouse suspicion."

"We could probably still communicate with relative security, but traveling as a gentleman and his lady wife will be much less complicated."

"Certainly." Less complicated for her, perhaps. He was sure she'd played the part of another man's wife more than once even before she'd become his. He, on the other hand, had never been anyone's husband but hers, and he wasn't sure he knew how to be that any more.

The skepticism must have been apparent in his voice because she turned to appraise him instead of his garments. "I believe you're up to the task. You have the education and bearing of a gentleman. And I have funds enough for any expenses we might incur...including a new wardrobe, should one be warranted."

She grinned and he felt his hands relaxing a little. At least she had a plan, even if she'd only give it to him in bits and pieces.

"You aren't going to travel the countryside looking like a laborer's widow," he returned. "Is a new wardrobe being readied for you?"

"No—I already have the necessary items. Cravats?" She picked up his three best shirts, the red waistcoat, and a navy blue cutaway coat, putting them in their own separate pile on his pillow. As he crossed the small chamber to search for a suitable neckcloth, she continued, "I have a coach and horses waiting outside the city, and my more expensive things are with them."

"Easier to blend in here if you don't look like a person of some fortune." That was how he walked The Liberties at night—dressed in the same manner as his neighbors, attracting as little attention as possible.

"Exactly so. See? You aren't so terribly out of your depth."

He returned with a length of white linen and handed it to her. "I suppose I do have some experience with deception. You know how hard I tried to belong at University." He had claimed to be a distant relation to the Earl of Waterford during his time at Trinity, keeping his actual origin to himself—a nobleman's kin, however distant, was more welcome than the son of a poor laborer.

"You did belong there," she said firmly. "And you may actually be his lordship's cousin. Wasn't your grandmother a Talbot?"

"She was. I always wondered if it wasn't her relations that paid for my education."

Joanna wound the cravat around her hand. "You never found out who it was?"

He shook his head, taking the bundled linen from her and putting it with the other approved articles. "Whoever it was, he or she does not want to be found. Perhaps Wellesley can discover the truth. Or perhaps he already knows." Michael paused, his hand still on the pile of clothing. "What does he know about me? Other than my penchant for taking nightly strolls around The Liberties."

"He knows that you're the Catholic son of a laborer, yet university educated. That your mother died at your birth, and your father was killed in a fight with his landlord when you were a boy." She reached out and took his hand, squeezing it with a gentle pressure. "He knows that you are neither anti-English nor anti-Protestant, but you favor Catholic emancipation. And that you fulfill every obligation you take on."

"He knows all that, yet he's invited me to become one of his trusted spies when I am his opposite in nearly every way? Why would he do that?"

The incredulity was clear in his voice, and he suspected it was written plainly on his face as well for Joanna gave his hand another squeeze.

"Because I vouched for you."

"You did?"

"Sir Arthur needed someone in Ireland in case the French made another invasion attempt, someone the people trusted. And I knew you would do anything to protect this city, this country."

"So you convinced him to make me a part of it."

"You're a good fit for this group, for the work we will be doing." Her gaze dropped to his chest for the briefest of moments. "And I needed a pretext to see you again."

That statement spawned a dozen more questions in his mind, but only one stumbled from his lips. "A pretext to see your own husband?"

"The longer I was away, the harder it became to return to you…"

Her fingers shifted against his, and he reflexively ran his thumb over the back of her hand to soothe her. "But fetching me to Wellesley gave you a reason to contact me again, without involving your pride."

"Yes."

"And here you are confessing it all to me anyway." Her hand was cold but steady in his grasp. If she was nervous or tense she wasn't showing it.

Not that he was surprised.

"There will always be secrets between us because of what we both are. But those are professional secrets, a necessity for people like us." She took a half-step closer to him, her sky-blue eyes focused on his dark ones. "But we kept too many other secrets from each other when we were together, and I don't want to make that mistake again."

"Nor do I. From this moment forward, we will be as open with each other as possible."

Michael was suddenly taken with the urge to kiss her, to seal the bargain as they used to do, holding each other close. But he shook off the idea. Even if they reconciled—and he was not at all sure they would—it was too soon to be that intimate with her. Instead, he released her hand and began gathering up his rejected clothing to return it to its case.

"What other preparations need we make for this journey?"

Two days later Joanna stood outside the stable housing her horses, ticking off the conditions of Michael's agreement in her mind one last time as she waited for him to arrive.

One: she'd introduced him to Cara Campbell the day before and had discreetly watched as he questioned Cara with the intensity of a French revolutionary in possession of a Royalist sympathizer. In the end he'd approved her as *pro tempore* Protector, spending much of the afternoon acquainting her with The Liberties in general and Hell in particular.

Two and three: Michael's close friend, Fion Nash, had agreed—with considerably less turmoil—to take over the children's reading lessons as well as the investigation into a missing will for Michael's one current client.

Four was still a bit of a loose end. Their visit to the tailor had gone well enough, with the proprietor promising to hire extra help to complete their order on time. But Joanna wouldn't know if he'd been successful until Michael appeared with the items.

The thought of him brought to mind another list she'd been mentally keeping—the list of things she needed to tell him before they reached Cork. Particularly the fact that she—

"Good morning, my lady." He approached her with a sardonic smile, setting down the small trunk he carried to remove his hat and bow deeply before her. Clad in rather plain breeches and tailcoat with just a hint of embroidered waistcoat peaking out, he looked like any other gentleman preparing for travel. But that smile lit his face, and the hat had tousled his dark hair.

For just a moment, Joanna wished she could kiss him hello and smooth his hair as if they were a happy couple.

Instead she curtsied with equal deference, dropping her gaze to his somewhat battered boots. She left off her Dublin accent for the more cultured tones of the English upper classes. "And a good morning to you, my lord."

A stable lad came to take the trunk, loading it onto the waiting carriage. Michael handed her in—with no outward sign of being affected by her touch—then settled himself on the rear-facing seat. "Tell me the rest of this traveling plan. How will we be known? Is there anything special I am to do?"

"Since there is no need to conceal who we are, we will simply be Mr. and Mrs. Devlin, a solicitor from Dublin and his doting wife." The carriage jerked into motion and Michael's knee brushed against hers. He again appeared not to have even noticed, and Joanna sighed inwardly. The next three days were going to be long indeed.

"That should be easy enough, then."

Hadn't she told him something similar only a few days ago? And it usually *was* easy to play the wife, to mimic the qualities the upper classes found pleasing in a woman. But sitting in the close confines of the carriage with the man she'd loved and left, it suddenly seemed a much greater task.

Fortunately, they had the business in Cork to discuss.

"There are nine others that Sir Arthur has invited from all over Britain. Some of them are peers with varying degrees of power, some gentry, and some who make their living with their hands."

He snorted. "Lords and laborers. That should be interesting."

"I think everyone will manage to get along in the interest of defending their country," she replied.

"I'm sure you're right. Am I the only Irishman?"

She stretched her legs a bit. "You are, though at least one of the lords has an estate in Ireland."

His head dropped back against the carriage wall. "Yes, that's nearly the same."

"I only meant that you may already know of one of them." Why was he being so contrary all of a sudden?

"Any women?"

And just like that he was back in her good graces. How many other men would even think to ask about female participants in this kind of organization? She stretched her legs again, sliding her feet across the floor until they bumped up against the far seat. "Only me, though I strongly suspect there are women who will indirectly be important parts of what we accomplish."

He slouched down in his seat, folding his hands together over his stomach. "What are we to accomplish exactly? What will we be gathering intelligence about?"

"The overarching theme is defeating Napoleon and his army, but you'll be watching and listening for anything that might compromise the security of the realm as you go about your usual business."

His mouth pulled into a smile at that. "'The security of the realm,' is it? That sounds mighty important."

"Not more important than ensuring the safety of your neighbors," she replied, patting his knee. "Just a way to do so on a larger scale."

"Yet, at least in my case, still working on a small scale." He hauled his feet up onto the seat, inches away from her hip. "You should have led with that when you first came to me."

"To appeal to your sense of protectiveness? Yes, that would have been a good way to get your attention." Not to be outdone—and because he looked exceedingly comfortable—Joanna untangled her feet from the striped carriage dress she wore and kicked them up onto the seat across from her, crossing her legs at the ankle.

He reached over and carefully re-draped her skirt, making sure her legs were covered all the way down to the ribbons on her shoes. Whatever had made him so cross before had apparently passed. "So basically, when I return to Dublin I'll resume patrolling The Liberties and just send word to Wellesley when I think I've come across something useful to him?"

"That's it exactly. I don't yet know if I am to be the go-between or if it will be someone else, but someone will always be in the area to convey messages to him."

"And to help evaluate the importance of the message?"

"Like a partner? Perhaps."

They debated the pros and cons of such a system until it was time to stop for a change of horses, then speculated on the practicalities of having messengers all over the country until the next change. By the time they'd run out of topics to discuss, the sun had nearly set and the carriage was pulling into the yard at what appeared to be a well-run inn.

"We're not traveling at night, then?" he asked, taking his feet down and looking for his hat.

She found it in a corner of the carriage, near where her bonnet had landed when she'd tossed it away. "No need for this trip. We have four more days before you're due in Cork and we can make it there in three while the sun is up. I'm not sure my driver would condone driving Irish roads in the dark, anyway."

"Not as smooth as some of England's," he answered with a short laugh. "The Romans never conquered Ireland, so they never laid roads here." He opened the carriage door and jumped down, letting the steps down himself before offering her his hand. "Ready, my darling wife?"

She allowed him to hand her out, then threaded her arm through his and pulled him close. "There is something I need to tell you first." In all their conversation that day, she'd completely forgotten about the list of information she meant to impart to him. Some of the items had been mentioned, but there was one rather important matter that had been neglected.

He covered her hand with his, large and warm. "What is it?"

"I didn't bring a maid," she whispered. "And I cannot get into—or out of—my clothing without help."

"The innkeeper's wife or one of the serving girls would suffice, surely?"

She went up on her tiptoes to rest her cheek against his, bringing her mouth a fraction of an inch away from his ear. "They would if I weren't carrying secret correspondence and weapons on my person."

Michael's whole body tensed beneath her touch. "It has to be me, doesn't it."

She kissed his check and pulled away, flashing him her most flirtatious smile. "Yes it does."

Chapter Three

THIS WAS NOT how Joanna had envisioned their journey to Cork.

The carriage ride had been pleasant enough, particularly after Michael got over his little fit of pique. The innkeeper had practically fallen at their feet when they entered his establishment, ordering meals and baths prepared, offering up anything else he thought they might want or need. The food, too, had been good, enjoyed in the private parlor with Michael and a few happy memories of meals past.

But there had been only the one room available, and the prospect of discussing sleeping arrangements discomfited her more than she was prepared to admit. Nor could she partake of the bath that had been brought up without Michael's help undressing, yet he stood motionless behind her as if the ties and buttons were some kind of mysterious puzzle.

"Don't be so missish," Joanna told him over her shoulder.

"I'm not being missish," he shot back. "I simply don't know where to begin. The last time I undressed you, your clothing wasn't this complex."

The last time I undressed you. That one phrase shredded her concentration and she could feel warmth creeping up her neck. Dear Lord, when was the last time he'd made her blush?

Probably the last time he'd undressed her.

"There are only buttons and ties. It shouldn't be that difficult."

He continued to stand statue-still behind her, and she imagined him watching the pink flush stain her skin. He used to kiss her where she blushed, brushing his soft lips wherever the color rose. Was he thinking of that? Was he fighting the urge to do it again?

"Michael."

"Yes, darling."

She choked back a laugh. His response had been almost reflexive, even after the years they spent apart— a far cry from the cold civility she had received from him only days ago. "At this rate, the bath will be ice cold by the time I get into it."

"Right."

She felt a tug at her waist as he untied the ribbon there, then a succession of smaller tugs as he made his way through the buttons down her back. Another tie negotiated, and the bodice of her gown fell into her waiting arms. She stepped out of it and her petticoat at the same time, draping them over the bed before once again presenting Michael with her back.

"Just laces?" she heard him ask.

Joanna nodded, catching the slightest whiff of lavender as he bent his head and set to work on her stays. She'd made him sachets of lavender before they were married to keep with his clothes, and the scent brought back a wave of memories. Not the big events, but the private moments they'd shared: curling up together before the fire on chilly evenings, clandestine looks exchanged across the room at social functions, kisses stolen while clearing the table after meals.

She'd never missed him so much as she did just then, and she mentally cursed the blackguard who had forced her away from her husband for five lonely years.

Her stays peeled away from her body and Michael stepped back, catching the letter that slid down her back. "What's this?"

"Part of that secret correspondence I mentioned." She turned and held out a hand, hardening her facial expression to shield her thoughts.

He placed it on her palm without comment, but watched with interest as she secured it among her belongings. "You were carrying it in your corset?"

"Who would think to look there?"

"Good point."

He continued watching her as she placed a foot on the bed frame, rucking up her shift to unstrap a sheathed dagger from one thigh before repeating the process with a small flintlock pistol on the other.

"That's new."

"The pistol? Yes." She handed it to him and adjusted her shift, noting that she was wearing practically nothing while he was still fully clothed. "I bought it the last time I was in London."

He turned it over, running a finger across the engraving on the end of the barrel. "You never used to carry a gun."

"I knew you didn't like them." She took it when he offered it back to her and set it on the bed with the dagger, then turned to him and began unbuttoning his tailcoat.

"And once I was no longer in your life, you decided my preference didn't matter."

"No. I needed the added protection of a firearm, and I'd promised you I would always keep myself as safe as possible." She circled around behind him and helped him slide off the coat, breathing in the smell of lavender once again.

"You were honoring your promise to me, even after you'd left me?" He turned around to face her with a furrowed brow, his mouth drawn down into a frown.

Joanna nodded. "I left that day on an assignment. You remember?"

"I remember." Those two words sounded more Irish than English and his eyes shifted to her shoulder.

She knew he was picturing the moment they'd said their goodbyes because she was picturing it, too—lying in his arms in their bed the night before she left, the down coverlet shielding them from the chill in the air.

"I was planning to return to you, Michael. I swear I was." She tilted her head, catching his gaze and holding it. "I promised you a full accounting after we are finished with Sir Arthur, and you'll have it. But let me say now that I didn't stay away willingly. I never abandoned you, never stopped believing we'd be together again." She reached up and stroked his cheek with the tips of her fingers. "I was always your wife, and I always loved you."

He cupped his hand around hers and brought it to his lips, brushing a kiss over her cold fingers before releasing them. "You told me that you would always be honest with me, and I dearly want to believe you. But I spent five years with no communication from you in any form, and that's going to be difficult to just let go of."

Strictly speaking, she'd sent a note a few months after her departure from Ireland. But since there had been nothing for years after that, she decided not to argue about such a small detail. She took a half-step back, putting some space between their bodies. "I know it is. And perhaps when you've heard my side it won't be so hard to believe. Until then, will you at least consider the idea that I didn't simply walk away?"

"I will." He said it without hesitation. For Michael, that was as good as a solemn vow.

Unless he'd changed in ways she was unaware of these past five years.

That night did not pass peacefully for Michael. He and Joanna slept side by side on the bed, she in her shift and he in his shirt, neither touching the other. The arrangement left him feeling confined and cramped, though physically he was neither. He kept waking up, afraid that he was laying on her long hair, that he had moved too close to her, that one of his arms or legs was somewhere it shouldn't be.

Why had Joanna told him her exile hadn't been voluntary? Why tell him that but nothing else? He finally gave up and grabbed his pillow, sprawling out on the hard floor in an effort to regain his sense of equilibrium. After two minutes on the wooden planks he knew he'd ache in the morning, but it would be worth it to calm his mind and relax his body.

The next thing he knew, he was being shaken awake as the sun was beginning to rise over the horizon. "Already? It feels like I just fell asleep."

"I didn't sleep so well, either," she confessed. "But we can always nap in the carriage."

Nap while his head banged against the window, she neglected to add. But it was better than sleep deprivation, and they needed to cover many miles today. Perhaps there was a pillow or two stored under one of the carriage seats. He pulled himself up from the floor and cast about for his clothing, distracted by the sight of Joanna standing before him holding her stays.

"Lace me up?"

Perhaps helping her into her clothes would trigger fewer emotions in him than helping her out of them had last night. It wasn't just the physical aspect of undressing a beautiful woman that got to him, though that had its own merits. That he had loved—and still did love—the woman in question with his whole heart, that he had her back in his life after a years-long absence, had thrown him off balance. It was like the past and the future had mixed together in some sort of porridge, and he couldn't tell the original ingredients apart anymore.

He rubbed his eyes and nodded. "Come here."

They ended up helping each other to dress and repack the items they'd taken from their luggage, for Michael's fingers were as sluggish with his own buttons and ties as they were with Joanna's. But they were both ready when Joanna's driver arrived to collect their things.

"Can we talk about why you slept on the floor last night?" Joanna asked, once they were on their way. "I thought we'd decided that the bed was big enough for both of us."

"I needed space," he replied with a shrug. When she narrowed her eyes in a hard stare, he clarified his statement. "I needed physical space to stretch out. It's been five years since I slept in a bed with another person, and I'm no longer used to sharing."

Her mouth opened as if she were going to speak, but no sound came out. She cleared her throat and tried again. "You never spent even a single night with...company?"

"No." His brows drew down over his eyes. "Why would I?"

"Because I disappeared without a trace for far longer than I told you I'd be gone. Because I could have been dead, or captured, or mistress to another man."

He was seated across from her once more, and slid his foot across the floor to touch hers. "You were my wife, and you continued to be so even when we were no longer in the same city. I'd never hurt you that way."

"I didn't...I was never unfaithful to you, either."

Before her words could sink in, the carriage came to an abrupt halt in the middle of the road.

"What—"

"Stand and deliver!"

The shout came from outside the carriage, and Michael sighed softly. "This is the disadvantage of traveling as a person of some fortune."

"There is a pair of carriage pistols in the compartment under your seat," Joanna told him in a low voice. "Do you still carry your cudgel?"

"Yes, I have it. How fast can you get to—" He was cut off when the door flew open and the barrel of a pistol appeared.

"Out of the carriage," a male voice ordered. "And keep your hands where I can see them."

Michael exited first, noting that the highwayman had been considerate enough to let down the stairs, then turned to offer Joanna his hand. She trembled as she took it, her eyes wide and darting around.

"What do you mean to do to us?" she asked in a tremulous voice.

Michael nearly laughed. She was no more afraid of this highwayman than she was of a kitten, but her performance was magnificent.

The barrel of the gun motioned them away from the carriage and Michael drew Joanna's arm through his, escorting her to the side of the road. "There, there dear, we'll be just fine as long as we do what the gentleman says." He shifted his gaze to the owner of the pistol, a younger man wearing finely tailored clothing. "Isn't that right?"

The highwayman smiled. "Just so. We only want your valuables, then you'll be on your way."

Joanna's hands covered her face and she began to sob. Michael slipped his arms around her, pulling her close and stroking her hair. "Shh, we'll be all right."

"There's another one with the horses," she whispered to him. "He's headed this way."

"Must have knocked your driver unconscious," Michael whispered back. "Or killed him."

"Let's hope not." She buried her face against his coat, holding his lapels in clenched fists and taking in great gulps of air as if she were trying to bring herself under control.

This second highwayman entered the carriage and Michael could see him searching the seats and floor. Looking for what? Joanna's jewels—with the exception of what she wore—were packed away in her baggage, along with her expensive gowns. The carriage pistols were finely made and would fetch a good price if sold, but the highwayman found then pushed away the box that contained them.

"Something isn't right," he murmured, kissing her forehead.

The first highwayman fished a canvas bag from the pocket of his tailcoat and opened it up, approaching Michael and Joanna with a friendly smile. "Let's get that jewelry off you, madam, and into my bag here. Sir, if you wouldn't mind assisting your lady?"

Michael set Joanna away from him and turned her around to undo the clasp of her necklace. "Just stay calm, my dear. I'm sure they are nearly done with us." He leaned down and kissed her temple. "I'll take this one."

She nodded and sniffled as he drew the necklace off. "Good."

Michael turned, holding out Joanna's necklace to the highwayman. When the robber reached for it Michael grabbed the barrel of his gun and yanked it out of his hand, crashing the butt against his head. Joanna disappeared—presumably to deal with the one searching the carriage—and Michael had to remind himself that the best way to keep her safe was to make sure she didn't have any unexpected assailants. His blow to the highwayman's head stunned the man but didn't knock him out so Michael tried again with his fist, wishing he could get to his cudgel—it was specially made to deliver a forceful blow without killing the recipient, and kept Michael from injuring his hands by delivering punches.

Fortunately, this recipient went down with relative ease. Michael retrieved Joanna's necklace and pocketed it before dragging the highwayman off the road and into the adjoining field. He'd wake up surrounded by vegetation which ought to disorient him, slowing him down should he try to return to his partner—the next best thing when there was no way to tie him up.

When Michael returned to the carriage Joanna had the second highwayman face down on the road, her little pistol pointed at the back of his head.

"Who sent you?" she barked.

"He didn't tell me his name. Only that I was to rob a coach carrying a red-haired lady and no footmen, and I wasn't to harm anyone."

"What did he want?" When the highwayman didn't answer, she placed her foot on the small of his back and pressed down. "What did he want?"

The highwayman groaned. "A letter. He said it would be for Sir Arthur Wellesley, and that it would be difficult to find. I've been robbing carriages all week looking for it."

"Just your bad luck that you chose us, then." He nodded a vigorous *yes*, squeezing his eyes shut as Joanna removed her foot from his back and knelt beside him. "Will you be robbing anyone else this week? Or ever again?"

"No, I swear."

She glanced up at Michael and acknowledged him with a smile. "Hold this for a moment, will you please?"

She held out the pistol and he took it from her, keeping it carefully aimed at the highwayman on the ground. Joanna first removed one of her shoes, then slid her skirts up to her thigh and removed her silk stocking.

"Let's get them tied up and get away from here."

She bound the highwayman's hands tightly with her stocking, then helped Michael drag him into the field with his accomplice, who was still unconscious. They bound him as well with Joanna's remaining stocking and headed back to the carriage.

"Well, you were right," he told her, taking her hand as they walked. "They didn't think to look there."

Chapter Four

MICHAEL SPENT THAT night on the floor of their chamber again, and consequently passed much of the following day dozing in the carriage. His dreams were jumbled and vague, but at one point he swore he felt a soft body cuddle up against his and smelled the fragrance of lilies in the air. The next thing he was aware of was Joanna's voice calling him back to the land of the conscious.

"We've arrived."

When Michael straightened in his seat and looked out of the window, he got an eyeful of summer sun sinking slowly toward the horizon. Rubbing his eyes and trying the other side of the carriage, he saw what could only be described as the largest red brick mansion in Ireland.

"What is this place?"

A footman opened the door and let down the stairs, standing by as Michael climbed out and handed Joanna down. "This way please."

Joanna slid her arm through Michael's as they followed the footman to the main entrance of the house. "Glanmire House. It belongs to the Earl of Hartland, who is one of the invitees."

"A building like this could house the entire population of Hell."

"And yet, for the next few days it will house only eleven secret informants and the servants employed here."

"And Sir Arthur," a male voice added as they stepped into the entryway. "I'm Hartland," he said, extending his hand.

Michael shook it. "Michael Devlin. And this is my wife, Joanna."

Hartland's gaze swung to Joanna. "Wait, you're married? I thought you were a widow."

"A widow?" Michael echoed. "You told him I was dead?"

She answered in a voice that might have been discussing a dinner menu. "It's a way to hide my identity. I don't use your name or mine, so few people know who I really am or who is close to me."

"I can see the sense in that," Michael admitted.

But Hartland was laughing and rubbing his hands together. "It's going to be fun introducing you tonight. My housekeeper, Mrs. McKenney, will show you to your chambers where you can refresh yourselves. We're having our after dinner port in the library if you'd like to join us."

"We will." Joanna answered before Michael could, taking his arm once again and leading him toward the staircase where the housekeeper waited. Once they were out of earshot, she leaned in and said, "He's a good sort, but it's best not to engage him too much when he's like that."

"Like what?"

"Gleeful."

"The library introductions are not going to go well, are they?"

She slipped her hand into his and gave it a squeeze. "They will be fine. By the time we get down there,

Hartland will have already told everyone about our marital status. They'll be curious about you, but once they realize that you have skills to offer the group they won't even remember that you have a wife."

Mrs. McKenney stopped at one chamber, opening the door and smiling brightly at Michael. "This is yours, Mr. Devlin. Your trunk is just there, and the bell pull is here. If you should require anything at all during your stay, just give it a tug."

Then she was leading Joanna away down the hallway, and Michael was left alone for the first time in three days. It was an odd feeling—though he'd lived by himself for five years he'd begun to get used to having Joanna with him again, talking to him, touching him. He'd fallen asleep the past two nights listening to the sound of her soft breathing, the rustle of the sheets when she was restless.

On the other hand, he wouldn't be sleeping on the floor anymore.

A knock sounded at the door and Joanna slipped in with a fresh gown draped over one arm. "Can you help me undress one more time? I need to give that letter to Sir Arthur."

"Even the maids here aren't to be trusted, eh?" he smiled, reaching for the row of buttons down her back.

"With the weapons, maybe."

"But not the correspondence." He worked in silence for a moment. "Who helped you dress in the first place? You were wearing your fine clothes when I met you at the carriage the first day we traveled."

"Cara Campbell. Lucky she was there, or you would have been dressing me in the stable before we departed."

There was an image he didn't need in his mind just before meeting a roomful of strangers. But instead of shoving it away, he tried turning the tables on her. "That would have been different. I don't think we ever got amorous in a stable."

Her shoulders rose a fraction as she sucked in a quick breath. "Well, there was that time in Kildare..."

"Our honeymoon? That was a meadow, not a stable."

"But there were horses nearby."

He laughed and began work on her stays. "Yes, there were. You said the piebald one was staring at us."

"I'm a spy—I like being unnoticed."

The letter slid out and he handed it to her, lacing her back up with a twinge of regret. Reminiscing about their tryst in the meadow had set his blood pounding in his ears...and other places. But there was work to be done this night, and he'd need a clear head for it. Nor did he want to entangle himself with this woman until they'd had a chance to sort through everything that happened between them. Joanna had said that her disappearance was forced, but what exactly did that mean?

He finished with her laces and helped her with the new gown, then allowed her to choose a clean waistcoat and breeches for him. When they were both ready, he offered her his arm.

"Shall we?"

"Let's go."

The library at Glanmire House was a vast room, the walls covered in floor-to-ceiling bookshelves, a large fireplace with logs and kindling ready to light, and various pieces of furniture made from walnut wood and leather scattered about the space. There were close to a dozen men clustered about the room in twos and threes, some talking in low voices, some with more animation.

"Ah, Mr. and Mrs. Devlin." The Earl of Hartland disengaged himself from his group and came to greet them, shooting Joanna a sardonic smile and placing a slight emphasis on her surname.

"My lord," she answered, dipping a curtsy with her eyes cast down in a show of demureness Michael suspected she didn't feel.

He managed his own bow. "Lord Hartland."

"Just Hartland is fine. Or Hart if you're feeling friendly." To Joanna he said, "Hoskins has something he needed to speak with you about. If you'd like to go see what he wants, I can introduce your husband around."

Joanna looked at Michael with raised brows and he answered with a tiny nod. He may not have had the training in social graces that Hartland had, but he could hold his own in a less formal gathering like this.

"May I present to you Mr. Laurence Fortescue of Oxford, Mr. Hugh Bannerman of Devonshire, and Lord Adam St. Peters of Kent. Gentlemen, this is Mr. Michael Devlin of Dublin." As handshakes were exchanged, Hartland continued, "You might also know him as the Demon of Dublin's Hell."

Michael fought the urge to both roll his eyes and hit the earl. Few people in the world knew that Michael was the Demon, and he'd wanted to keep it that way. But these men were supposed to be trustworthy, and it was clear by the smirk on his face that Hartland was doing his level best to shock his guests.

"I didn't know Dublin had a Hell," Lord Adam commented. "Nice."

"Not really," Michael replied. "But it's home."

"Wolfgang of the Seven Seas and the Marquis of Thorston, or should I say Thunder," Hartland continued, gesturing as he approached a pair of gentlemen glowering at each other a few feet away, "Meet Michael Devlin of Dublin. Also known as the Demon...and Mrs. Perkins's husband."

"She's married?" Wolfgang growled, echoing Hartland's own earlier words.

"She is," Michael told him with more force than he'd meant to use. Wolfgang of the Seven Seas? What was that all about?

"All right then."

Hartland moved to the last group without even checking to see if Michael was with him. "Lord Adam Bateman of Berkshire, Mr. Colin Hoskins of Kent, this is Michael Devlin of Hell."

Lord Adam arched a single brow. "Hell?"

"It's a area of Dublin," Michael clarified.

"Not a good one, then," Hoskins said with a laugh.

"That's why I'm there," Michael replied. "To make it better."

Another gentleman joined the group, offering first a bow then his hand to Michael. "Captain Grant Alexander."

Michael took his hand and shook it. "Michael Devlin."

"Ah, Joanna's Michael. She mentioned you when she delivered my letter."

Michael struggled to keep his mouth from falling open. "She did?"

"She was excited to be going home to her husband. I didn't realize you'd also been invited here. I'm pleased you could join us."

She'd been excited to come *home*? Michael wondered if that was the word Joanna had actually used, or if it was Alexander's interpretation. She'd never lived in the rooms he occupied now, but perhaps it was the notion of love and partnership that constituted home for her.

It certainly had for him.

After everyone had retired to their chambers for the night, Michael stole quietly down the hallway and knocked on Joanna's door. Though why he was sneaking around he wasn't sure—Hartland had indeed made sure the entire assemblage knew she was his wife.

A soft, "Who is it?" answered his knock.

"Michael."

The door opened a moment later and she motioned him to come inside. "I was going to have one of the maids help me tonight..."

"Help you? Oh, with your clothes. That's not actually why I'm here."

"It isn't?"

Michael thought she sounded disappointed. Had she been looking forward to reenacting the meadow scene? "I was hoping you'd go over the guest list with me, and tell me a little more about each man here."

"I can do that." She motioned toward a sofa positioned at the foot of the bed. "Shall we sit?"

He seated himself beside her after she was settled. "They all know about my role in The Liberties, but I realized that I know little about any of them outside of their names."

"Well, Mr. Fortescue, Captain Alexander, and Major Bannerman are in the army, though in Fortescue's case that's rather sensitive information. They aren't in the same unit, nor do I think they've ever crossed paths before now. Wolfgang and Mr. Hoskins are commoners—Hoskins is an archery master, and Wolf is...well, Wolf is a pirate. When he's not at sea he spends most of his time skulking around places of ill repute."

Michael turned to look at her, his eyebrows reaching for his hairline. "Why on earth was this Wolf asked to be a part of a secret intelligence-gathering group, then? And why does he have no other name than 'Wolfgang'?"

"His name is a long story, but he's proved— repeatedly—that he can be trusted. And besides, he visits places no one else here has ever been to."

"That makes sense. It was the reason I was invited, too, wasn't it? Because I go places no one else goes."

"It was."

Her arm brushed his as she reached out to smooth a wrinkle from her skirts he didn't see. "It was why each one of you was invited. There are ten of you gentlemen and me—while our interests and locations may overlap in some cases, we each have a unique quality or two that makes us valuable to Sir Arthur and the struggle against Napoleon's agents."

"What's Hartland's unique quality?"

"Other than his money? He's actually rather brilliant at designing and building things."

"What kind of things?"

Joanna slipped her arm through Michael's and took his hand, resting her head against his shoulder. "Whatever he wants."

Michael closed his eyes and he savored his wife's touch. "That's a handy sort of man to have around."

"So are you."

"Am I?"

"Yes." She lifted her head a moment to press a kiss to his shoulder. "Will you stay with me tonight? I'll sleep on the floor or here on the sofa, and you can have the bed. I just feel odd about spending the night in separate rooms."

"I don't know, Joanna..."

"Everyone knows we're married, so there won't be a scandal."

He pulled away from her to look her in the eyes. "Since when do you care what other people think?"

"I don't," she answered without hesitation. "I only meant that there wouldn't be any repercussions. One can't ruin one's own wife."

"That is true," he grinned, stroking a fingertip over her cheek. Then he glanced back at the big bed behind them. "I suspect we could both sleep comfortably there. Even with my need to spread out."

"That's one benefit of having Hartland host," she told him with a smile. "Well appointed accommodations. I suppose that means you may help me undress after all."

"How well do you know his lordship?" Michael asked, rising from the sofa and shrugging off his tailcoat.

She rose along with him, taking his coat to drape it over the arm of the sofa and reaching for the buttons of his waistcoat. "I was in contact with him more than the others, making arrangements for our stay, so perhaps there's a little more familiarity there. Why?"

"I don't like the way he was looking at you."

She pushed the waistcoat off his shoulders and down his arms, turning him around to remove it from his body. "He's a rake. He looks at every female that way."

"He shouldn't. And you aren't every female."

He heard a light laugh. "Are you jealous, Michael?"

They traded positions, and he went to work on the buttons running down the back of her gown. "No, it isn't jealousy. It's protectiveness, I think. Though I'm not sure if I even should feel protective of you."

"Because we were apart for so long?"

"And because you can take care of yourself. I always knew that, but it wasn't until I saw you interrogating a man you'd wrestled to the ground that I *knew* it."

She stepped out of her gown and laid it atop his coat on the sofa. "It's easier to have faith in something you see with your own eyes."

"That's not faith, that's fact."

They were both silent for a time while he dealt with the laces of her stays. But when she'd removed the garment, she turned to him. "Did you believe that I would come back to you?"

"No. But I always hoped you would."

She took his hands in hers and kissed each one in turn. "And now that I have?"

"We still have a lot to discuss. But I am thankful that you're safe and unharmed." He adjusted his grip on her fingers and gave them a little squeeze. "Were you ever worried about me? That you'd come back to Ireland and find me gone...or dead?"

"Every day. There was no way I could obtain information about you without putting you in danger, and that drove me nearly to distraction. I'd lie awake at night and imagine all sorts of scenarios, none of them ending in our happy reunion."

Michael allowed his heart to overrule his head for once and slid his arms around Joanna, pulling her close. "I wouldn't say our initial reunion was happy, but we've managed sufficiently these past few days. We're both whole and uninjured, too."

She rested her cheek against his shoulder, cinching her arms about his waist. "I am glad I no longer have to take either of those pronouncements on faith."

He kissed the top of her head, the gesture borne of genuine affection this time rather than the need to convince a criminal. "So am I."

Chapter Five

"If you would all please be seated, we will begin."

They were gathered in the formal dining room, the eleven people Sir Arthur had invited milling about until the man himself brought them to order. Joanna found herself sitting between Lord Adam Bateman and Lord Thorston, trying to keep her eyes from darting down the table at Michael. She had slept entwined with him the previous night, somewhat awkwardly at first but with more ease as the night went on, in what turned out to be the best rest she'd had since her arrival in Dublin. She hadn't had a chance to speak with him this morning, though, as Sir Arthur had arrived earlier than planned and let it be known that he was ready to attend to business.

"Each of you has been called here because you have proven yourselves honorable, trustworthy men, and because you are needed—needed by your King in defense of the realm, as well as by each other to continue your individual work. Mrs. Perkins will have already told you the purpose of this assemblage is to pass along information you might come across that would be of use in the fight against the so-called Emperor of France and those of his ilk. That is indeed the case."

Joanna saw Michael frowning at the use of her alias. Perkins was etymologically equivalent to Pearson, but she supposed it was strange for him to hear his wife—a wife that had once been the person closest to him in the world—called by a name that wasn't really hers...or his.

"As you go about your regular activities," Sir Arthur continued, "you will simply remain alert for such information. When you discover something relevant, you will compose a letter and convey it to one of five messengers I have engaged to bring your correspondence directly to me. They will be stationed in various parts of the country, so one should be near to you at all times. This way, your letters will travel faster and more securely than by post."

Lord Thorston sighed beside Joanna and muttered, "He likes speech-making as much as my brother does."

Lord Adam straightened in his chair. "What if you are not available? You are about to disembark for the Peninsula in anticipation of a direct confrontation with Bonaparte. It is therefore plausible you may find yourself in the midst of a major battle. In such circumstances it is highly likely we will be unable to communicate with you."

"Arrangements have been made to forward all correspondence from this group to Mrs. Perkins, wherever she is at the time, should I be unreachable."

"Will we be allowed to correspond with each other?" Fortescue asked.

Sir Arthur looked at each of the faces around the table. "You would want to do that?"

"Certainly. Some of these men are scientists, as I am, and we could benefit from each others' counsel. Some are involved in other occupations that might prove useful to me, or where I might provide something for them."

Sir Arthur's eyes shifted from man to man as their heads began to nod, including Michael's. He'd said connections made within this group might be helpful, and here he was making them despite his initial resistance and his dislike of Hartland.

"I know some of you are involved in attempting to curb various crimes in your localities," Bannerman said from across the table. "Perhaps we could alert one another if one of us discovered something nefarious planned to happen or an unsavory character was traveling to another's city or village.

Choruses of "yes" and "excellent idea" circled the table while Sir Arthur looked as if he were trying to figure out when he'd lost control. Joanna grinned and let her gaze drift again to Michael, who looked much more comfortable than she had thought he would be. His posture was straight but not stiff, one open hand rested on the table, and she could practically hear his mind whirring as the discussion went on.

Sir Arthur held up his hands, palms out in a supplicating gesture. "It seems there are many benefits to you all keeping in contact with each other." He waited for the room to quiet before going on. "I will ask that you reserve the use of the messengers for extremely urgent business only, if you use them at all among yourselves. All other correspondence not involving me will be sent through the regular post. Mrs. Perkins, you will collect the direction of each man and compile a list to be distributed. Each man will memorize then destroy his copy before departing."

Joanna merely nodded, but she knew she'd be spending the next day or two copying out that list. Would Michael help if she asked him to?

"Are we to have a name?"

Joanna leaned forward to see who had spoken, and discovered Hartland sitting at the foot of the table with an impish grin.

"A name?" Sir Arthur responded.

"Yes, like the Royal Scots Greys or the 95th Rifles."

"Those are army regiments, Hartland," Alexander countered before Sir Arthur could. "We are not a military unit."

"We certainly are not. But it will be easier to refer to this group if we have a name. Wellesley's Watchdogs?"

Michael had been quiet thus far, but he spoke up at that. "We shouldn't be referring to this group at all except to people who are a part of it, and we all know who the members are. If the group has a name, then someone can tie us all together. And if something happens to one of us, we would all be in danger."

"Mr. Devlin makes a good point," Sir Arthur said with what looked like relief on his face. "You will have no formal name. You are not spies on foreign soil, but it is infinitely safer if no one outside this room knows about our affiliation."

The ten men at the table became more sober at this pronouncement, but heads were again nodding. And Michael—a working class Catholic—had won a moment of respect from a wealthy Protestant.

Joanna smiled to herself, her shoulders loosening and letting go of tension she hadn't realized was there. It had indeed been wise to include Michael in this group.

She had only to convince him to include her in his life.

They spent two more days at Glanmire House working through the practicalities of Sir Arthur's system—Where exactly would these messengers be? And how would they be contacted? What if one of the group traveled away from home?—and producing copies of the list containing each person's direction.

Joanna and Michael spent those nights in their separate bedchambers, too weary when they retired to discuss anything of importance. Joanna decided that, despite sleeping fitfully alone in her bed, it was probably for the best they had some time apart. They'd been together practically every moment since leaving Dublin nearly a week ago, and she needed to decide just how to explain her five-year disappearance.

On the third day they departed together in her carriage; she needed to pay a visit to a particular someone in Belfast and he agreed to accompany her as far as Dublin. They sat side-by-side on the front facing seat, his hat and her bonnet keeping company opposite them. But neither of them spoke, and every time the carriage swayed Michael was careful not to bump her, not to touch her at all.

Well then, why not tell him about her missing years now? If he was already disenchanted with her, what did she have to lose?

"His name was Simon Burroughs."

Michael's head swiveled around, his brown eyes meeting her gaze. "What?"

"Simon Burroughs. He's the reason I didn't come back to you five years ago."

This time his whole body turned and one arm when up along the back of the seat cushion. "So it was a man."

She turned to face him. "But not like you think."

"All right then, I'm listening." His tone said he was calm and open-minded, but the lowered brows and down-turned lips told a different story.

"I told you the truth in the note I left, that I had a mission and planned to be back in a month or two. The mission itself was straightforward and I completed it with no problems. The trouble began when I stopped at an inn one night as I was making my way back to Ireland."

She paused there, scanning his face for any hint of what he might be thinking. Whatever was going on in his mind, though, was now carefully hidden behind a neutral expression.

"A man came to sit with me as I was eating dinner— yes, I was eating in a private parlor," she said, interrupting herself before Michael could, "but the innkeeper came to me, saying this man professed to know my husband and wondered if I might take a message to him. I was wary, of course, but I consented and the man was ushered in to my parlor."

"Simon Burroughs?"

"His lackey. He said his master knew that Perkins wasn't my real name and that I was no lady."

Michael's jaw clenched, and Joanna wondered if he even realized his was gritting his teeth.

"There was a letter, too, containing my full name and the fact that I was in Sir Arthur's service."

"How did he know that? What did he want?"

"That was precisely what I wanted to find out."

His hands clenched into fists. "You went after him, didn't you? Without even telling me."

"At first, yes," she admitted, carefully controlling her breathing as she spoke. "I thought I could track him down quickly, discover his source of information, and put an end to his game."

"You tracked him down, but it wasn't quick."

"No. Burroughs kept himself well hidden. It took me three months just to find his name."

Michael's body was rigid now. "And in those three months you didn't think to send me word that you were alive? Or any time after that?"

"But I did," Joanna replied with a frown. "Just once. I knew it was a big risk—if Burroughs found out you were the Demon he'd ruin you, or worse. I knew you'd be worried, though, and sent a note to your cousin Anne thinking that she would pass it on to you. It was vague and probably unhelpful, but I wanted you to know I was well and that I'd come home when it was safe."

The anger in his face vanished. "You sent it to Anne? When?"

"It must have been late July, maybe early August. A few months after I'd left Ireland."

"Joanna, Anne was arrested near the end of July that year. She was accused of conspiring with her employer to help plan the United Irishmen rebellion and jailed as a spy."

Joanna's hand covered her gaping mouth, then dropped into her lap. "I didn't realize... I told her in the note not to reply. So you never—"

He shook his head. "She disappeared after they released her. I haven't seen her since."

They sat unspeaking for several minutes, listening to the horses' hooves striking the road. One letter sent in five years certainly wouldn't exonerate Joanna in Michael's eyes—nor would she have forgiven him if the situation had been reversed. But it did prove that she hadn't walked away without a care.

Would that be enough to rebuild a marriage?

Probably not. But perhaps it was enough to start the process.

"I assume Burroughs is no longer a threat." Michael's tone was steady but his words carried just a hint of his natural brogue.

She wanted so much to touch him, but she didn't dare. Not yet. "He is not."

"And we are both safe?"

She nodded. "From him."

"Are there others he was connected to that we should worry about?"

"Not that I am aware of."

He fell silent again and she sat back against the cushions, trying to give him both physical and psychological space to think through the situation.

"Is Wellesley's intelligence gathering ring the only mission you're currently working on?"

"No." She was prepared for anger at her answer, but was taken aback when he cracked a smile instead.

"I know better than to ask about what you *are* working on."

Good. That was progress. "What have you been working on?" She knew there would be some regular criminal the Demon always had his eye on, and remembered how he'd liked to discuss possible strategies with her.

"The head of the Ormond Boys has been trying to stir something up with the Liberty Boys."

"Again?" She chuckled and felt her shoulders relaxing. It was good to know some things never changed.

"Always. Catholics and Protestants, butchers and weavers, constantly feuding. I don't think they even know why anymore."

Joanna watched some of the tension ebb from his muscles and she reached for his hand. "I hope we don't follow their example."

"I hope not, either," he said, turning over his hand so it was palm to palm with hers. "But what are we going to do?"

"Do you despise me?"

His warm brown eyes met her blue ones. "Of course I don't."

She took a deep breath and let it out slowly. "Then perhaps we can begin again."

"As husband and wife? I don't think I can jump right back into that relationship."

"You—we—won't have to. I will need to travel some to continue my...work. But what if I made my home in The Liberties," she laced her fingers with his, "and spend my off duty time courting you?"

That elicited a surprised laugh from Michael. "You want to court me?"

"Yes. I'm the reason we've been apart these years, so I should be the one doing the wooing."

"Do you have any idea how to court a man?"

She gave him her most inviting smile. "You will just have to wait and see."

Chapter Six

Dublin, September 1808

MICHAEL SAT IN the larger of his two rooms ostensibly listening to a small group of his students reading a book, but his mind kept wandering toward the door in anticipation of Joanna's arrival. They had made plans to walk out together to enjoy the setting sun before the Demon went to work for the night, and she had insisted on coming to him. He wondered vaguely if she was going to bring him flowers again, too.

When the children came to the end of a chapter, Michael rose and began to stack up the books they'd been using. "That's enough for today."

"It's still early, Mr. Devlin. Can't we read just a little more?"

"The story is just starting to get interesting!" another chimed in.

A third child, a boy named Daniel, grinned broadly at Michael. "Miss Pearson's on her way, isn't she?"

"She is." Michael couldn't stop his own smile from growing, despite the use of Joanna's maiden name. She had thought it easier to explain her presence to his neighbors—who knew nothing of their marriage or subsequent separation—as a new sweetheart rather than a rediscovered wife. He had agreed, but found himself nearly overcome by the urge to correct people when they didn't call her Mrs. Devlin.

Michael must have had a dreamy look on his face, for the children began to giggle and Daniel patted Michael's arm. "I'm sure she'll offer for you soon."

Michael laughed, swatting Daniel's hand away. "You think it's funny that Miss Pearson pays calls to me instead of the other way around. But if you met a lady as beautiful and fascinating and capable as she is, you wouldn't mind if she did the calling."

"My mam says it isn't proper for a lady to visit a man in his rooms," a girl called Jane announced.

This time Michael smothered his smile. "Your mam is absolutely right. That's why Miss Pearson and I always go out walking in public or have a proper chaperone."

That seemed to satisfy all the children and they bounced to the door, scattering down the staircase toward their respective homes. Michael gathered up the pile of books and began to put them in their customary places on the bookshelf when he caught the slightest hint of lilies drifting in from the open door.

"You're early," he said without turning around.

"I couldn't wait," Joanna replied. He could hear the purposefulness in her steps as she crossed the small chamber and slid her arms around his waist, planting a soft kiss between his shoulder blades.

He turned, throwing a brief glance at the door to confirm she'd closed it behind her, and scooped her up to bring her mouth level with his own. She laughed and settled her arms about his shoulders, leaning in for a deeper kiss.

Her mouth was cold against his, tasting of lemons and sugar. But soon enough it was as warm as her hands stroking his cheek, feathering through his hair, and he pulled gently away. "Any more of that, Miss Pearson, and you'll have to propose marriage to me."

She was grinning as he set her back on her feet. "Any more of that, Mr. Devlin, and I just might."

After a few moments deliberation—and another kiss or two—they opted for a walk around nearby Christ Church Yard and what had been the Four Courts before they were moved to new buildings closer to the River Liffey. Strolling arm-in-arm they headed down Christ Church Lane, through the old arch with the wooden devil statue that gave Dublin's Hell its name, and up the narrow passageway toward the Viking-built cathedral.

"How did things go in Belfast this time?" Michael asked.

"Much better. I finally discovered the name of the man behind the attempted robbery on the road to Cork."

"Who is he?"

She flashed him a cheerful smile. "Hugh Bodkin."

"I take it you've run up against this Bodkin before."

"I have, and one or two of his cousins. They're common criminals—no training, no subtlety, no finesse."

"In other words, they aren't as good as you are." He bent down and pressed a quick kiss to her lips before they emerged from the lane into the openness of the Yard.

She blinked at him a moment before replying, "Definitely not as good as I am. But you're getting better. I didn't anticipate that at all."

"I'm very motivated to improve." He managed the words with a straight face, but his mouth curved into a smile immediately after he spoke them. "So does this Bodkin have any ties to Simon Burroughs?"

"Not that I've found." She'd been worrying about that same question for weeks, and the creases forming on her forehead told Michael she wasn't completely satisfied with the current answer.

Her hand gripped his arm and he laid his hand atop it, giving it a small squeeze. "If they exist, you will find them."

"I'm just afraid I'm going to waste time trying to make connections that aren't there."

"Could your Miss Campbell help? You said she lived in Belfast."

Joanna nodded. "We talked about it just before I left to return home."

"Home to your husband," Michael replied. "That's what Captain Alexander said you told him when you delivered Wellesley's summons to him."

She laid her head against his shoulder then pressed a kiss to his arm. "Home to my husband, who is masculine enough to let me escort him about and bring him gifts." She straightened, then sighed softly. "I do wish you'd consent to accompany me once in a while when I travel, though I understand why you feel you can't leave Dublin."

"That is one of the things I love most about you, wife of mine." They'd reached the shadow of the cathedral and he tugged her close to the ancient stone wall. "I never need to make explanations to you because you understand the way my mind and my heart"—he untangled their arms and guided her palm to the center of his chest—"work. I am freer with you than I am without you."

She stood up on her toes to meet his kiss but he tilted her chin up and bent down to her, encircling her in his arms. Her lips were warm this time but still sweet, and he suspected it had more to do with their love for each other than any lemonade.

"Perhaps one day I will go with you," he whispered, his mouth a hair's breadth from hers. "We do seem to travel well together."

She laughed at that and threw her arms around his neck, stealing another kiss before he could draw back. "But next time you get to carry the secret letter in your underpinnings."

"And you'll help me hide it?"

"Every single time."

He dropped feather-light kisses on her hair, her forehead, her nose before finding her mouth once more, channeling all the feelings swirling though his body into the kiss. He was caught between sorrow for the time together they'd lost, joy in having her back in his arms, and uncertainty about what lay ahead for the two of them. So when Joanna began to giggle, Michael was surprised and slightly offended that she had not been swept away by his attentions.

"What's so funny?"

"We are having a very private moment up against a church." He must have given her a funny look because her giggle blossomed into a laugh. "Didn't you tell the children we went about in public for propriety's sake?"

"And here we are in an intimate embrace for all the city to see. That's not exactly appropriate, is it?" His lips pulled into a grudging smile. "I also told them we had a chaperone when we were together indoors, so that's two lies I told today."

She combed her fingers through his hair again, massaging gently as she spoke. "We had one the night we went to the theater."

"Your driver doesn't count."

"Then I suppose we should be more careful."

He didn't even have to tell her how important his neighbors' sensibilities were to him, and he felt his heart swelling with gratitude and love. "I was thinking that, when we're ready, we might also have a small wedding ceremony...again."

"And invite everyone who thinks we are unmarried? Don't you think that's taking the ruse just a bit too far?"

He kissed the corner of her mouth and rested his cheek upon hers. "We could invite our closest friends and celebrate our new beginning, the future together that we've regained."

She tightened her arms around him. "What a beautiful idea."

"And perhaps your Miss Campbell could pay a visit to Dublin again while we took a little trip."

"No meadows this time."

He felt her smile against his cheek. "As you wish, my lady."

She drew away, sliding a hand across his face and down his neck, letting it come to rest on his chest. "A second wedding we shall have, then, and a second honeymoon as well. I look forward to becoming Mrs. Devlin again."

"And I look forward to your proposal." Her eyes went wide and he grinned. "You said you wanted to do the wooing—the proposal is part of that."

"Perhaps I can find your cousin and ask her for your hand."

Joanna was smiling, but Michael sobered a little at her comment. "If you could find her, I'd be indebted to you forever."

"It would be my pleasure to reunite the two of you. Though it would be even better if we worked together to find her."

"We should add that to our list of things to accomplish. As you go about your work for Wellesley, and I gather information around Dublin, we should also start a serious search for Anne together. My solo investigation has gone nowhere."

Her smile returned, though it looked slightly wistful now. "We will find Anne, and celebrate our second wedding with her. I promise you that."

"From your lips to God's ear."

"We're in the right place for that," she replied wryly. "Do you want to go in and say a prayer for her?"

He shook his head and took her hand, leading her away from the old cathedral. "I won't exactly be welcome in a Protestant church. We can go to St. Audoen's later."

"As you wish, my lord," she said lightly. "As long as you don't sneak off and go without me."

That coaxed his smile to return. Even before their separation he was wont to spend a large portion of his time alone, and though she'd teased him about it from time to time, she'd never begrudged him a minute of it. "Not this time."

"Good. I missed too many important things when I was gone, and I never want to miss another."

He stopped in the middle of the open Yard and took both her hands in his. "Let's promise each other right now that we will do our utmost to never miss an important event in each other's lives."

She stepped closer and kissed him, heedless of any passersby. "I swear it with all my heart, Michael. I'll do everything I can to be with you when it matters most."

She had allowed the tiniest suggestion of her native French accent in her words, and he reciprocated with a little of his Dublin brogue. "And I with you. Always."

He wrapped her in his arms, sealing the bargain with a series of kisses. Just as they'd done countless times before.

The Heart of a Hero Series

No Rest for the Wicked by Cora Lee

Only A Hero Will Do by Alanna Lucas

Once Bitten by Aileen Fish

Lightning Strikes Twice by Jillian Chantal

No Hiding for the Guilty by Vanessa Riley

The Marquis of Thunder by Susan Gee Heino

The Good, The Bad, And The Scandalous by Cora Lee

The Archer's Paradox by Ally Broadfield

The Missing Duke by Heather King

The Mercenary Pirate by Katherine Bone

Chapter One Excerpt from:

Only A Hero Will Do
The Heart of a Hero Series

Chapter One

London 1811

ELIZABETH STROLLED INTO the stuffy, overly perfumed, and crowded ballroom. Some of the finest families of the ton were in attendance this evening. She pretended she had not a care in the world, but all the while took note of those around her.

Within the mass of well-dressed lords and ladies, Lord Fynes caught her eye, offering a slight nod toward the less crowded terrace. This was the signal she'd been waiting for all night.

Promenading the perimeter of the dance floor and heading toward the terrace, Elizabeth feigned interest in the quadrille, but continued to glance sideways at the portly Lord Baxter, the man she was to keep an eye on this evening.

Elizabeth had been given the tasks of attending social functions where Lord Baxter was present and taking note of whom he interacted with, and any other odd behavior. If it weren't for Lord Fynes' cryptic note about a stolen missive needing to be deciphered posthaste, and Lord Baxter's sudden decision to attend Lady Caper's ball this evening, she'd still be at home pretending to be ill. But these new developments took precedence over avoiding social obligations.

Elizabeth's mother, however, was thrilled with the last minute alteration to the evening's plans, promising Elizabeth would have a splendid time and declaring that, by the end of this season, her daughter was sure to have an offer of marriage. There was only one problem with her mother's theory; Elizabeth had no interest in marriage. Truth be told, she had never been a starry-eyed debutante setting her cap at handsome men. Not that she wasn't interested in the opposite sex. She just did not want to give up the life she'd worked so hard to build. She wanted to serve her country and help bring down Typhon, the Legion's mysterious and deadly enemy.

Despite the Legion's efforts to apprehend Typhon over the past several years, he'd continually managed to evade capture. After the last informant had turned up dead, all traces of Typhon and his miscreants had vanished, until last month when the Legion had received word from the Earl of Hartland stating he had uncovered information regarding influential members of the ton who were sympathetic to Typhon's anti-British cause. Lord Baxter's name was at the top of the list.

Lord Fynes' exuberant voice rose above the chatter, breaking into Elizabeth's reflections. "Miss Atwell, what an unexpected surprise it is to find you here this evening. I do hope your family is well. Is Lord Atwell in attendance?"

She flicked her fan open. "My father is not in attendance, but is well, thank you, Lord Fynes." Glancing over her shoulder, she noticed Lord Baxter heading their way. The continual mopping of his brow, combined with his anxious expression and jittery movements, added to Elizabeth's suspicions. She didn't know if Lord Baxter suspected anything, but there was no time to contemplate the possibility. Lowering her voice, she spoke between waves of her fan. "What news?"

"Standard assignment to be delivered by Cap..." Lord Fynes halted his sentence before pasting a wide smile on his face, and in a boisterous voice exclaimed, "Lord Baxter! I was hoping we'd meet again this evening and continue our engaging discussion about the benefits of sea air on one's constitution."

Lord Baxter's face paled as little beads of sweat outlined the corners of his brow. "Oh yes, of course, sea air... one's constitution... perhaps later." He gulped the words down with force. Pulling out a white cloth from the edge of his coat, he wiped his brow with much force. "Quite warm this evening," was all the man could mutter before waddling away. It was difficult to believe the always-discomposed Lord Baxter could be involved in anything nefarious. Elizabeth suspected the man's immense wealth had attracted Typhon's attention.

Masking her thoughts, Elizabeth resumed the role of guest at Lady Caper's ball. "I had best be returning to my chaperone. It was a pleasure to see you this evening, Lord Fynes."

"Give your father my regards." Bowing slightly, Lord Fynes uttered under his breath, "Captain Alexander...tonight." Without further adieu, he took his leave, disappearing imperceptibly into the festive crowd.

Although she'd been deciphering messages for Lord Fynes since she was an adolescent, Elizabeth had only recently joined the ranks of the Legion, a secret organization created to destroy anything or anyone that might compromise the security of the realm.

Thankfully her father had not objected, and her mother had no knowledge of her surreptitious activities.

The daughter of a viscount simply did not risk life and limb. No, the daughter of a viscount was expected to marry well, provide heirs, and know the latest on dits. The daughter of a viscount was expected to behave herself, do what she was told, and not be in possession of a weapon of any sort. Elizabeth had absolutely no interest in being that daughter.

She forced her best smile and prepared to wait. Patience was not her strong suit. Scanning the room, she looked for the man she'd heard so much about but had yet to meet. She'd been following his impressive military career for several years and was anxious to make his acquaintance.

When Typhon had struck again a few weeks ago, Elizabeth was not surprised to learn Captain Alexander had been appointed to discover the identity of the man who had been slowly undermining British authority and weakening general confidence. Typhon's ultimate goal was to destroy the crown. His ever-expanding organization knew no boundaries, and it was the Legion's responsibility to bring him to justice. Elizabeth had no doubt Captain Alexander would be the man to accomplish such a feat, and she wanted nothing more than to be part of that team.

Anxious energy coursed through her limbs. If she stood still much longer, she might scream. Across the room, she spotted her chaperone, Lady Carteron—her recently married and dearest friend, Amelia— and decided to join her.

Elizabeth thought it quite ridiculous that, at the age of six and twenty, she still needed a chaperone. She did not quite understand how her younger friend provided any additional protection because of her recent change in marital status. Her mother and father, however, did not share her sentiment.

Girlish giggles followed by excited hushed whispers drifted over from a group of young ladies. The room quieted as all heads turned toward the entrance and the mysterious newcomer. It seemed as if every lady in attendance had noticed his arrival and were prepared to throw herself in his path.

He had the stature of a military man, proud and confident but not arrogant, and stood at least a head above most of the men in attendance. There was an air of danger and mystery about him that Elizabeth found intriguing. Could this be Captain Alexander?

Elizabeth strolled over to Amelia, but kept her eyes settled on the handsome gentleman in a dark blue coat. "Who is the impressively tall man?"

His gaze swept through the ballroom, resting on Elizabeth. Rapid flutters pattered against her chest as her eyes locked with the mysterious newcomer, catching her off guard. She quickly turned her gaze as if looking for someone.

Amelia leaned in and whispered, "That is Captain Alexander. He's recently returned from Glanmire House."

Oh dear. Elizabeth had heard he was handsome, but he was a veritable Adonis!

"And standing next to him is Sir Simon," Amelia added.

Oh, so that is Sir Simon. Elizabeth had heard the numerous tales about his bravery, and his reputation with the ladies. She tried to suppress a giggle. Sir

Simon's renown was second only to the Earl of Hartland's. She had no interest or time for rakes and scoundrels.

"They've been the best of friends since childhood."

Amelia always seemed to know everything about everyone. Calling her a gossip would have been a gross understatement. Except for the one not-so-minor flaw, Amelia would have made an excellent agent. However, she was instead a loyal friend who, without a doubt, would never betray Elizabeth's trust. Even still, Elizabeth had always acted with extreme caution regarding her other life. Few knew the truth of her association with the Legion, and she meant to keep it that way.

She happened another glance at Captain Alexander, who was now engaged in conversation with Lord Capers. His stoic features gave nothing away. She suspected that beneath the rigid and all too handsome façade was intelligence and compassion. There was just something about his aura that told her he was a good man. A good man and an excellent spy.

"What do you know of Captain Alexander?" Elizabeth questioned without thought, wanting to know more than just of his military career. Not that she had any interest in the Captain beyond the professional, but she'd often found a person's past influenced their present course.

Take herself, for example. Elizabeth had always been told she would never be able to fire a pistol, or hit a target with an arrow, or have a place in a man's world. But the moment her late grandfather had revealed his secret, she'd instantly known the path her life would take. She was going to prove every naysayer wrong.

Amelia took in a deep breath and began to rattle off the facts. "He was a sickly child, often bedridden. Both his parents died when he was still fairly young and has no other living relatives. He has served in the military, but no one knows much about his service apart from his strong sense of honor and duty. He has traveled extensively and speaks multiple languages. Rumor has it that his late grandfather had amassed quite a fortune in trade and acquired Brookhurst, a lovely property near the Peak District. He's not married." Elizabeth eyed her friend, about to ask if that was all the information Amelia had on Captain Alexander when she added, "Oh, and he's thirty years old and has managed to keep all romantic entanglements out of the gossips' ears. Other than that, his life is shrouded in mystery."

"Yes, shrouded in mystery." Somehow Elizabeth was able to hold in the laughter. Apart from extremely personal details, Amelia had covered all the basics.

How would she approach him without raising suspicion? Did Captain Alexander know who she was? Perhaps he already applied to the master of ceremonies for an introduction.

She was contemplating her next course of action when Mr. Cokinbred, one of many fortune hunters in attendance, sauntered to where her and Amelia were standing.

"Lady Carteron," Mr. Cokinbred said in a polite, if not slightly condescending tone, before turning his attention to Elizabeth. "Miss Atwell, it is a pleasure to see you this evening." His smile widened revealing a set of ill-maintained teeth. "May I have the pleasure of the next dance?"

Propriety dictated she accept, but conformity was not a common word in Elizabeth's vocabulary. "I thank you for the offer, but I am rather tired at present."

Mr. Cokinbred's face turned to an unflattering shade of red. Under his breath he muttered, "Good evening," before storming away, clearly displeased with Elizabeth's refusal.

Amelia leaned in and, with a teasing whisper, said, "Your mother will be none too pleased when she hears of your refusal to dance."

Ignoring Amelia's comment, Elizabeth shifted her attention back to the dance floor. The orchestra was in place and guests were lining up for the next set. Sir Simon had already secured his dance partner. She noticed Captain Alexander standing alone off to one side, surveying his surroundings. Despite the lack of gentlemen in attendance, he had yet to ask a lady to dance. Perhaps he was not as much of a gentleman as she'd first thought him to be.

A group of colorful young debutantes paraded in front of Elizabeth, obstructing her view of Captain Alexander. How was she to catch his eye if she couldn't even see him? By the time the young ladies flitted past, he was nowhere to be seen.

She flicked open her fan for the second time in a span of fifteen minutes and began fanning herself fervently. It was becoming quite the undesirable habit.

"Are you alright, Elizabeth dear?"

Elizabeth clutched her chest with her other hand and let out a long sigh. "It is rather warm this evening. I fear I may be taking ill."

Amelia raised a single delicate brow, her eyes narrowing with a dubious look. They'd been friends a long time and Amelia instantly knew when Elizabeth was up to something. "I find it rather pleasant this evening," she teased.

Keeping with her charade for those who might overhear, Elizabeth continued to fan herself. "I believe I just need a moment's reprieve. Do you happen to know the way to the ladies' retiring room?"

"Down the hall." Amelia pointed before adding in a hushed tone, "The same direction in which Captain Alexander disappeared a short time ago."

Elizabeth snapped her fan closed. "I don't know why I even bother."

"Because I am your dearest friend and want to help." Although Amelia did not know the specifics of Elizabeth's involvement, she had always suspected it had something to do with the government. On numerous occasions she had tried to weasel it out of Elizabeth, all in good fun of course, but Elizabeth had never conceded. Amelia had promised on pain of torture and death never to reveal what she suspected. And she had never given Elizabeth cause to doubt that promise.

Elizabeth smiled. "Thank you. I won't be long."

Edging along the perimeter of the crowd, Elizabeth trudged toward the ladies' retiring room under the charade of illness. When she reached the hall, she resumed her normal pace.

Elegantly dressed ladies paraded up and down, ready to resume their husband- hunting antics, their giggles echoing off the gilded mirrors and fluted columns.

Even before she saw him, she felt his larger than life presence. Captain Alexander.

She strolled around a column, pretending to admire a rather grotesque orange, green, and gold floral vase. Captain Alexander was leaning against the wall, partially hidden from view by another column and a decorative pedestal. Her earlier assessment of him did not do him justice. He was like a Greek god, but more handsome and far less arrogant.

"Have you noticed that Mr. Devlin's bays are mismatched?" His soft deep voice sent a tingle all the way down to her toes, catching her off guard for a moment.

What was wrong with her? Despite the many attempts by the ton's most handsome rakes and scoundrels, she'd never been this distracted by anyone before.

Breathing in deeply to steady her nerves, she swallowed the hard lump in her throat. Neither attempt was of any use. Ignoring the intense fluttering in her heart, she replied in code, "Yes, I believe he acquired them in Dublin."

Captain Alexander surveyed both directions before nodding toward a partially opened door. Elizabeth glanced behind to ensure no one was watching and then followed him into the dark drawing room.

It took a moment for her eyes to adjust to her surroundings. Slowly, a couple of sofas flanking a large table came into focus.

Captain Alexander came up besides her, turned and faced the door. The aroma of fresh soap and leather encircled Elizabeth, infiltrating her senses. They were common enough scents, but on him were intoxicating and far too intriguing.

"It's a pleasure to finally meet you, Miss Atwell." His words were a mere whisper. "And quite an honor that you side-stepped Mr. Cokinbred and left your chaperone to meet with me." The teasing tone in his voice made her insides tingle. For the first time in her life she understood why her sisters all swooned at the sight of a handsome man.

"I do not care for the rules of the ton, especially when they are far inferior to protecting and safeguarding our country. I believe you share this sentiment, Captain Alexander?"

A slight laugh escaped his lips. "Yes, I would assume Lady Carteron informed you of who I was and told you my entire life story?"

"Only the highlights." Elizabeth confessed with a nervous giggle. Focus on the task at hand. "I understand you have something for me?"

Captain Alexander took her gloved hand and slipped a folded piece of paper into her palm, then closed her fingers over the small missive. The motion seemed intimate, inappropriate, and all too enticing. A strange inner excitement coursed through her veins.

"Guard this well. Lord Fynes will be calling on your father first thing in the morning."

Captain Alexander did not wait for her response, but disappeared further into the darkness of the drawing room. A cool breeze and another hint of fresh soap and leather drifted through the space, followed by the soft click of a door closing.

Elizabeth took the folded letter and smoothed it across her chest, tucking it into her dress and nestling it on the outer curve of her breast. The intense beating of her heart was a steady staccato against her hand. She sighed deeply, letting her head fall back against the wall.

"Elizabeth," a soft voice questioned from the hall.

At least she wouldn't have to pretend to be flustered. Captain Alexander had aided her sufficiently with that unwanted response.

She edged off the wall, smoothed her hand across her chest, ensuring the missive was securely hidden, and then strolled toward the doorway. "In here, Amelia."

Before Elizabeth reached the door Amelia pushed it open, allowing candlelight from the hall to filter into the drawing room, casting eerie distorted shadows across the walls. "What are you doing in here?" She glanced about as if expecting to find someone.

"I just needed a quiet moment." After her brief encounter with Captain Alexander, that was the truth.

"You are missing all the dancing. I promised Lady Atwell I would not let you be a wallflower this evening. You already turned away Mr. Cokinbred. If you don't make an effort, your mother will not ask me to chaperone again, and then where will you be?"

Elizabeth had never been a wallflower in her entire life. Her decision not to be social had nothing to do with shyness, but an intense unwillingness to abide by the ton's rules. But Amelia was right. She had to make an effort, or else risk having her mother at her side at each and every future event of the season until she was married off. A fierce shudder replaced the delightful tingling she'd felt only a moment ago.

She sucked in her breath and forced her best I'm-enjoying-the-evening smile. She might look the part of a viscount's daughter, but inside beat the heart of a spy.

Grant was relieved to be back in the quiet of his room. He found social functions more draining than marching in the rain through ankle-deep mud. Sighing deeply, he enjoyed the silence that afforded him time alone with his thoughts. The evening had not turned out as expected.

When he'd informed Lord Fynes about the missive he'd recovered and whom he believed had written it, he'd expected his superior to handle it himself. But when Grant received orders that he was to deliver the coded missive to Miss Atwell, he'd expected an old spinster who dabbled in amateur mysteries. However, instead of an elderly woman on the cusp of death, a lady who could bring any man in a room to his knees had greeted him. Not just greeted him, but enticed him in a way no other female had before.

Sinking into the warm comfort of the leather chair, Grant's thoughts strayed to Miss Atwell. She had turned down a dance and left her chaperone's side, all to accept a missive? Her large brown eyes held an intelligence far beyond her youthful years, and then there was her luxurious brown hair that glistened beneath the candlelight, not to mention her voice...her voice was pure heaven. She was the type of woman dreams were made of— entirely perfect, but far out of Grant's reach. Miss Atwell was the daughter of a viscount, lest he forget that not so minor detail.

How was it even possible the daughter of a viscount was the Legion's top decoder? And why hadn't he known about her previously?

From Lord Fynes he had learned she was able to decipher codes faster than any man, and also had a knack for puzzles. It was a talent that made her highly valuable to the organization in this game where time was of the essence.

When he'd pressed Lord Fynes for further details about Miss Atwell's background and qualifications, he'd been warned that the information was classified. Although Grant understood the need for discretion, he detested all the secrecy. It made it difficult for him to do his job and protect his team when he didn't have all the facts.

He swirled the brandy in his glass, watching the liquid slowly ripple to a gentle stop. Lifting the glass to his lips, he inhaled the fragrant aroma before taking a long, slow sip. The fiery liquid burned as it traveled down his throat and settled into his gut. Why would a lady born to privilege want to do such work?

Grant suspected he could drink all night and still not be rid of the image of the beautiful and intelligent Miss Atwell. He was far too intrigued by her, and not just in the physical sense.

End of excerpt *Only A Hero Will Do* (The Heart of a Hero Series) by Alanna Lucas

Chapter One Excerpt from:

Once Bitten
The Heart of a Hero Series

Chapter One

June 1812
London

LURKING IN THE shadows backstage of the Theatre Royal in Haymarket, Lord Adam St. Peters watched unnoticed as the so-called Mr. Tilney performed his lines in the farce, *Vicar Pauley's Petulant Pig*. Behind the curtain, stagehands shuffled pieces of furniture and carried painted walls to be moved into place at the end of the act. With all the activity around him, Adam was free to study the actor, the man he knew as Mr. Boiselle. The man who caused the death of Lord Fitzwilliam St. Peters, Adam's uncle.

Dust, powder, and who knew what else billowed about with each movement around Adam, taunting him to sneeze and draw attention to himself, but he swiped the back of his hand across his nose to stifle the urge. Under the lights onstage, Boiselle swished around like a drunken fop with weak ankles, wavering on his feet. The flap on one of his shoes was loose and the buckle, covered with paste diamonds, threatened to slip off. All in all, Adam decided watching to see if that jeweled piece fell off was much more entertaining than the actor himself.

As much as he'd prefer to leave, Adam couldn't risk letting Boiselle out of his sight. There had to be some covert reason the spy would conceal his identity with such a public façade as an actor. One of the stagehands or audience members likely passed information during scene breaks or after the production.

The hair on the base of Adam's head, directly above his elaborately tied cravat, began to itch. He scratched absently. Again, those short hairs tickled his skin, and he scratched with more force. When the itch continued, he dug beneath the cravat to relieve the discomfort. And promptly felt a sharp sting on his finger.

He shook his hand, ripped off his cravat and swiped his neck to get rid of what he was certain was a spider. Several of the workers paused to watch his primal dance, bringing Adam to his senses. His face heated with embarrassment—grown men weren't afraid of tiny creatures, and drawing attention to himself was the opposite of what he wanted. Straightening his waistcoat, he wrapped the neck cloth as well as he could without a mirror, while keeping an eye on the stage.

The finger where he'd been bitten itched horribly, and in the light slipping past the edge of the curtain he saw it burned bright red and swelled remarkably. When he was a youth, he'd received some sort of bite that had left him gasping for air until he fell asleep, frightening his mother horribly. Cursing silently, he hoped the sweeling on his finger would be the extent of his body's reactions.

Luck wasn't with him. Adam began to wheeze, his lungs allowing only small breaths. Damnation. He needed cool air, needed to go outside, away from this crowded, dusty space, but he couldn't let Boiselle share his secrets again.

Bracing himself against the wall, he fought his body, willing himself to remain calm. He took slow breaths as deep as he could, but each brought on the need to cough. He was growing dizzy—he had little choice but to step into the alley. Turning toward the door, he tripped over a box of properties, knocking into a burly man who tugged on a thick rope dangling from above.

"Watch out, you soused slug," the stagehand barked in a loud whisper.

Adam could do nothing but stagger on, tugging at his cravat as if it was the cause of his breathing difficulties.

A sweet voice spoke from over his shoulder. "Are you all right, sir?"

He waved her off, wanting only to escape.

"Let me help you. Mr. Billups has the same complaint. Sit here and I'll bring him to you."

Having little choice, Adan collapsed on the small wooden chair she guided him to, and prayed she knew of what she spoke. The notion was foolish—unless the man was an apothecary, why would he have medicines on hand?

Mere minutes later, the young woman led a thin old man to his side. The man held out a pipe. "This will help," he said.

Adam waved the man away, gasping, "Can't breathe. Can't smoke."

The woman—who looked rather fair in the dim light, he couldn't help but notice—placed her hand on his arm. "Trust him. I've seen Mr. Billups gasping one minute and breathing calmly the next."

Since his breaths weren't coming any easier, Adam gave in. He put the pipe between his lips and, when Billups held a lit match to the bowl, he inhaled. The acrid smoke made him cough, drawing scolding looks from the people working backstage, and he fought to take it in. After a few puffs, the change came slowly, but soon he could breathe. Adam caught the woman's eye. "Thank you. And thank you, too, Billups. What is this I'm smoking?"

"Stramonium. It stops me from wheezing."

He'd never heard of it, but the herb obviously helped. He handed the pipe back to the old man and straightened in the chair, allowing himself to draw in more air.

And then it hit him. He'd lost sight of Boiselle. Adam could hear him onstage, but what if another actor has passed a note within a prop, or changed the dialogue subtly with a code? How easily Adam might have failed his family. He must take better care. Boiselle would be charged as a spy or Adam would die trying to expose him.

Mary Jane Watson couldn't take her eyes off the young man in front of her. Handsome was too weak a word for the way he looked. Dashing, suave, a bit proud, and quite clearly a gentleman despite his worn clothing, he was pleasing to speak with. What was he doing here? Most of the dandies who waited for a tête-à-tête with one of the actresses did so from a box seat in the audience. He wasn't dressed as finely as the noblemen who often visited the dressing rooms, but he certainly held that air of privilege.

"Are you looking for someone? Miss Clarke, perhaps?" she asked. "You may wait in her dressing room; it's what most of her gentlemen friends do."

His gaze darted quickly to the curtain and he shifted nervously. "Er, no."

"Simply a fan of theatrics, I take it. Wouldn't the play be more enjoyable where you could see the entire stage?"

He jumped to his feet. "Thank you for your assistance. You're truly an angel for saving my life. If you'll excuse me..." With that he strode off in the direction of the dressing rooms.

Strange, strange man. He piqued her curiosity. She had nothing to do until Susan Clarke needed to change for her next scene, so she followed him.

The gentleman's destination came as quite a surprise. He paused outside Mr. Tilney's room, not one belonging to the actress, and looked up and down the hallway before stepping inside. She had no excuse to offer if she knocked on the door, so she went to Susan's room and waited just inside the doorway, listening for Mr. Tilney's return. On previous occasions, she'd heard yelling between the actor and an unknown man. She'd assumed there was a matter of debts owed, but that might be her imagination. Believing Tilney had dallied with a married woman and her husband had come to seek revenge was much more exciting. Yet the argument never came to blows, so a debt seemed more likely.

Sighing, she chided herself for her wicked fancies. Hearing the dialog onstage night after night left her believing her life was too dull. She didn't want anything to happen to herself, but being a witness would be very exciting. Her mother would scold her for wishing ill on anyone, yet whether or not Mary Jane imagined it, those things happened. She wasn't planning to cause anyone harm.

From the stage, Susan recited the line that warned of the end of the scene, when she and Mr. Tilney would exit the stage. The gentleman remained in the dressing room next door, heightening Mary Jane's attention. She turned to prepare the costume for the next scene, knowing she was overreacting. All that would happen was the typical argument with a quick, but loud resolution to the situation. By tomorrow, no one would remember.

Then she heard the creak of the door. She rushed to peer into the hall. The gentleman stepped out of the light from the dressing room and slipped stealthily toward the exit. Now this was what she longed for—excitement! She tiptoed after him, ducking behind a large stage property when he glanced back.

He went out the door, closing it quietly behind him. When she reached it and looked outside, he was nowhere in sight. Disappointed yet again, she returned to Susan's room and went back to work.

The play ended late in the night. While most of the stagehands and actors had left, Mary Jane cleaned a spot of rouge off the gown Susan wore in the final scene, made certain the jewelry was safely tucked away, then blew out the candles. Her maid, Bridie, came out of the other actress's dressing room and followed her to the exit.

The theatre was quiet, as was the street where the patrons had awaited their carriages. She preferred it that way, allowing her to leave unnoticed. She'd tipped a hackney driver quite handsomely when she first went to work backstage all those months ago, so he'd return for her each night, and he never failed to see her safely home. Luckily, Bridie knew her place and wouldn't scold her the way Charlotte would have. Her friend agreed to keep Mary Jane's escapades a secret, torn between envy and concern. Just so long as Papa never found out what she did when he believed her asleep in her room, her life would be enjoyable.

Before they reached the end of the alleyway, a man stepped out of the shadows and waited for her to draw closer. Heart racing, she slowed and moved toward the opposite wall, her petite maid hovering just behind.

At that moment, Mary Jane wished she'd listened to Charlotte.

"I don't mean to frighten you," the man said, his face hidden in shadows below his hat. "I only wanted to thank you."

Recognizing the stranger from backstage didn't make Mary Jane feel any safer. Just because he spoke like a gentleman didn't mean he couldn't be a scoundrel. "There's no need."

He fell into step but kept toward the wall on his side, leaving a few feet distance between them. It wasn't quite enough to slow her heart rate. "Are you an actress?"

"No."

"I assumed you were." He lifted one finger to his lips and sucked on it, then shook his hand. "You're pretty enough to be."

Subtlety wasn't his strongest quality. She wasn't a lightskirt; she wouldn't dally with him no matter how handsome or rich he was. She didn't respond.

"You work at the theatre, then. I've always wondered how one finds a part in a play."

No one had tried that method to befriend her—or seduce her. She wasn't a fool, regardless. "One would audition."

"Yes. Yes, of course. When would the next audition be?" He continued to flex his hand as though he'd injured it and appeared to be quite distracted.

"Sir, I'm not the person to ask. Nor am I the type of woman you seem to hope. You're wasting your time."

"Forgive me, again. I hadn't meant to imply—" He stopped mid-sentence and picked up his pace, leaving her behind.

What an odd sort he was. Part of her wondered what he really sought, and why he thought she'd know. Anyone who'd gone home before her could answer as well as she had.

Foremost in her thoughts was the possibility of an intrigue. She could imagine many interesting reasons for his actions.

However, she was too tired to think any more about him. All she wanted was to crawl into bed beside her cat and sleep. Any further entertainment must wait for another day.

End of excerpt *Once Bitten* (The Heart of a Hero Series) by Aileen Fish

Chapter One Excerpt from:

Lightning Strikes Twice
The Heart of a Hero Series

Copyright © 2017 Jillian Chantal

Chapter One

Oxford, England, Summer 1812

HESTER HALE, DRENCHED to the skin with her gown plastered to her body, darted out into the rain again to untangle the line she had tied to her kite. The wind wasn't cooperating at all with her experiment.

"Come back to the shelter. You know we need to keep this ribbon dry and I don't want to be the one holding this key if this crazy idea of yours works," Jane Gresham, Hetty's closest friend called out, her voice almost lost in the noise of the storm.

Hetty wasn't going to stop what she was doing. No, not at all. She'd been waiting for this moment for a while now. If the great Benjamin Franklin could make this happen, why shouldn't she be able to do the same?

Realizing her kite string was wrapped around one of the hedges near the outbuilding where she and Jane were conducting their—well, Hetty's—experiment, she breathed a sigh of relief. This would be easy to tend to and get the kite back into the air.

She made quick work of her task and slogged back to Jane.

"Your mother is going to disown you." Jane raised her hand in a motion to indicated Hetty's attire. "I believe that to be one of your better morning gowns. It's a sodden mess now. Your maid will never be able to make it presentable again."

"Never mind that. See all the beautiful lightning in the sky? It's popping and snapping everywhere and I want to take advantage of it."

Jane tossed the key on the string she still held. It landed on the ground with a soft plop.

Hetty let out a little shriek. "Don't get the ribbon wet. Mr. Franklin's biographer said a dry ribbon was essential. That's why I'm under this covered shed in the first place. I would've thought the experiment would work better out in the weather, but I read that article about Mr. Franklin and I think that's why I failed in the past."

"I cannot comprehend why you even want to do such a thing as this. It makes no sense. Why not tend to your needlework instead?"

"Because this is interesting. Needlework is dull." Hetty held the key in her hand with the ribbon dangling below it.

"At least needlework is done inside by a warm fire, not out of doors in the midst of what has to be one of the worst storms in Oxfordshire's history."

"You do tend to exaggerate, my dear Jane."

"Admit it. This is not something we, as well-bred young ladies, should be engaging in."

"Never. We're gaining knowledge." Hetty shook the ribbon in Jane's face. "All young ladies should work to challenge their minds."

"That doesn't sound like something you learned from your governess."

"No. I actually learned it from my brother's tutor."

Jane blanched and looked as if she were going to choke. "What was John's tutor teaching you?"

"Don't be silly. He wasn't talking to me. He said it to John."

"About young ladies?"

"No." Hetty nudged her friend's shoulder with her own. "About young men. I was merely using his words to illustrate my point."

"You'll say anything to get your way."

"But you still want to be my friend so I can't be that bad."

"Someone has to make sure you're kept out of trouble." Jane laughed. "Although right now, it seems as if I'm not doing that so well. Your gown is well and truly ruined and I somehow think I'll be blamed for it."

"Never mind that. My mother will blame us both. She never thinks you're the one to lead me astray. I do that quite well all on my own." Hetty sneezed.

"Oh no, now you're going to catch your death. If you get a lung infection, I will be in trouble. Come inside and change into some dry clothing."

Lightning lit up the yard. Hetty took a step toward the outer edge of the covered area. "No time for that. Look. Now is the moment I've been anticipating."

"Don't go back out there. It's too dangerous." Jane tried to grab her friend's arm, but it was so slick with rain, her hand slipped off.

Hetty stuck her head out into the rain at the same time a bolt of lightning hit the ground a few inches from her.

"Get in out of the rain. Now, please," Jane pleaded.

Ignoring her friend, Hetty pushed her windloosened curls off her face, held on to the key and waited, hoping for the same effect Mr. Franklin had with his experiment.

Several more times, the sky lit up all around them.

At the moment, it seemed the storm was going to move on with no results for Hetty, a large boom of thunder shook the ground. A tingling sensation started at Hetty's fingertips and ran up her arm almost to her shoulder.

She turned to face Jane, but before she could say anything, another boom of thunder erupted. The sensation in her arm returned, more intense this time.

As she rethought her plan to try to harness the thing called electricity and made a move to set the ribbon and key on the ground, a huge bolt of lightning hit the key and threw her backward. The last thing she was aware of was her body shaking all over before everything went black.

The next moment, she found herself looking up into Jane's terrified eyes.

Hetty tried to sit up, but was so dizzy she had to put her head back on the soggy ground. Ground? What was she doing down here?

"What happened?" she asked.

"I think you were hit by the lightning. You were standing there and then your body moved as if someone struck you in the stomach with a sharp weapon. You fell and hit your head on the dirt. It scared me since you weren't moving and had your eyes closed. It was as if I wasn't here."

"My mother is definitely going to be upset with me now." Hetty sat up, held on to her aching head and plucked at the soaked fabric of her gown. "When this was only wet, that was one thing but now that it's drenched and muddy, there's really no help for it."

"Will you quit worrying about your gown and worry about yourself. Didn't you hear me tell you that the lightning hit you? Hard?"

"I'll be all right. Mr. Franklin was."

"I don't think he got a strike like that. That really was something to see. In fact, I can hardly believe you're still alive," Jane said with a quaver in her voice.

"Alive?" Hetty wanted to laugh off her friend's words, but the way her head was hurting and her ears were ringing, she wasn't sure it was all that amusing. Could she have really died from what happened?

"Yes. Alive. You didn't see yourself. It was quite the worst thing I've ever seen. Your entire body seemed to light up from the inside and the force of the blow knocked you off your feet. Even your blonde hair seemed as if it were on fire. It actually turned a shade of gold."

"It seems I'll survive, though." Hetty tried to stand, but found her legs were weak and wouldn't cooperate. Her hair hung limp and wet around her face in what had to be a catastrophe.

"Do I need to go get someone? Can you manage?"

"I think I'll wait a few minutes. I'm sure I'll be fine once I have a chance to rest a moment."

"You'll be even muddier and wetter. Let me help you." Jane held her hand out for Hetty to take.

Once she was on her feet, Hetty tested her ability to put one foot in front of the other. Her knees shook, but by holding on to Jane's arm, she was able to move forward.

"How do you suggest we return to your house in this downpour?" Jane asked.

"I think we'll have to wait it out here inside this cowshed. It'll at least be warmer in there than out here." Hetty sneezed again. "My head is hurting."

"You're getting sick. We can't stay out here."

Hetty, still holding on to her friend's arm, said, "Please assist me inside."

They entered the small outbuilding. Hetty was relieved to see the mound of hay she thought would be there. It would at least allow some warmth for the two of them until the rain abated enough for them to make their way across the lawn to the main house.

She stepped over to the hay and sat, pulling Jane down with her. "We can rest here for a while." Leaning back, Hetty rested her aching head on the golden straw. Sneezing again, she smiled at her friend. "This time it's the hay, not the wet."

"You say that, but I bet you'll be ill."

"There's nothing to be done about it now." Hetty closed her eyes. She just needed to sleep. She was sure her head would be better if she could take a short nap.

"You're scaring me. Your face is pale and I'm afraid that lightning strike damaged your insides."

"If it did, there's not much we can do." Hetty didn't open her eyes. Why couldn't Jane be quiet? Her voice seemed to be getting louder and shriller by the moment.

"I still don't know why you had to do this. Why you have this need to perform these experiments."

Hetty didn't respond. She hoped if she pretended to be asleep that Jane would eventually believe she was and stop talking.

The rain on the roof sounded as if it were slowing even more. Maybe they could return to the house soon.

Truth be known, Hetty wished she were able to ring for her maid and have a hot bath delivered.

Jane suddenly went silent, but Hetty didn't have the energy to look to see what she was doing. It was enough that she stopped speaking.

The next thing she heard was some type of scuffling noise. Was it a rat? Surprisingly, she didn't care. All she wanted was warmth. Sweet, blessed warmth. Snuggling further into the hay, Hetty tried to cover herself with it like a blanket.

The scuffling noise got closer. It was now accompanied by what sounded like whispering.

Someone suddenly scooped Hetty up from her nest in the hay.

With effort, she opened her eyes. And was met with a pair that looked exactly like her own. John. Her brother.

"Is she all right?" Jane's voice again. Too loud.

"She's feverish and covered in hay and mud. I can't believe she's still behaving as if she were a child of twelve when she is old enough to be married with a child of her own."

Hetty swatted at John's chest. She tried to tell him to hush, but no words came out. What was wrong with her? Was she dying? She didn't think so, but she sure didn't feel right. It was like some sort of fog had settled over her. A terrifying, deep, dark fog. And then everything went black again.

When she woke, Hetty was in her bed, in a thick night rail and with a blazing fire heating the room to an almost unbearable level.

Glancing around, she spotted her brother in the chair by the fireplace with a book in his lap. "John? Why are you here?"

"Mama said someone needed to stay with you to be sure you didn't try to escape and try some other means to kill yourself."

Hetty sat up and adjusted her pillows. "I am quite sure Mama said no such thing. You're here to lecture me, I know it."

"It seems I'm the only one who is attempting to prevent you from continuing to behave like a hoyden."

"I know I'll be taken to task by both of our parents as soon as they know I'm feeling better. There's no need for you to do the same. I've heard it all before."

"Then why can't you act more dignified?" John stood and stepped over to her bedside. "If you could've seen how upset Mama was when I brought you in covered in mud and only the Lord knows what else, you would rethink your conduct."

"You're always so serious and condescending. Ever since our real Mama died all those years ago, you've acted as if you're responsible for me. Father's remarriage and bringing in a new mother for us should've changed that. Let them be our parents. I don't need a second father anymore."

"But you did when he wasn't happy and was drinking all the time. I find it hard to stop trying to help you so you'll have to accept it, I'm afraid."

"I don't have to like it, though." Hetty slapped her palm on the mattress. "And now that I'm awake, I realize I'm starving. Did I miss dinner?"

"You sure did. Your friend Jane was frantic when she came and asked me to help bring you into the house. Once we had you settled, Mama and I took her home in the carriage. They held dinner until we returned. I imagine Cook would be happy to find you something now that you're awake."

"Please ring for my maid since you're closest to the cord."

"Only if you tell me one thing first."

"To sing for my supper, you mean?"

John shrugged. "No, please don't sing. Remember, I've heard you do so and it's not pleasant."

Hetty let out a deep sigh. "What do you want to know then?"

"Are you playing at these scientific experiments to try to get Laurence Fortescue's attention?"

"I'm not playing. I'm serious about it. I'm interested in the world and how it works."

"And you're also interested in a certain man who teaches at Oxford University. No need in denying it. Everyone knows it." John stood and walked over to the cord to call for the maid. He tugged on it. "Even though you didn't tell me the truth, I'll get you something to eat. There's no fun in letting you starve."

"That's so kind of you." Hetty said with a laugh.

"Not really. I'm only doing it because if you die from your exposure to the elements or from starvation, the mourning period would be inconvenient to my plans to visit Tattersall's this week."

"You're needing a new horse?"

"Need is a relative term, dear sister." John turned to leave. "I'm sure you'll be fine in the morning and will be able to come down to greet Father at breakfast."

"I'll probably have chocolate in bed since my head is still aching." Hetty realized the pain behind her left eye had intensified and things were a little blurry as well.

Hoping she hadn't done some kind of permanent damage to herself with the kite experiment, she rested her head on the pillows again. "Ask Mary to bring me something soft. Maybe bread and milk. I don't think I can hold anything else down."

John strode back to the bed. He reached out and touched Hetty's forehead. "You seem overly warm. Should I fetch the doctor?"

"No. I think I crave some sleep. At least I hope that's all it is."

"Jane said that lightning bolt hit you hard. I think we should bring in Doctor Waverly."

"If I feel this bad in the morning, then we can."

The door opened to Hetty's maid.

"Yes, Miss?" Mary asked.

"My sister still isn't well and would like some milk and bread."

Mary curtseyed. "Right away, sir."

Once she was out of the room, John said, "You're looking even worse by the moment. I'm not going to wait for the morning to send for Doctor Waverly."

Hetty tossed the coverlet from her bed and placed her feet on the floor. "Let me show you I'm fine. Don't bother the doctor this late in the evening."

When she stood, her knees wobbled and she almost collapsed. Hetty reached out for the coverlet to help steady herself, but missed.

Before she hit the floor, John grabbed her by the waist and lifted her effortlessly to the bed. "Stay here. You can't worry about inconveniencing the doctor. He's right down the road and expects to be called out to people's homes on occasion."

"I really believe I'll be fine by morning."

"I'm going. You won't talk me out of it." John left the room.

Hetty thought again about rising and asking one of the staff to stop her brother from his task. She didn't want to see the doctor, mostly because she didn't want to have to confess what she'd done to get herself in the condition she was in. It would be another thing to have her family add to the list of grievances they already had against her.

Before she could make the attempt, her maid returned with her meal. "Miss, I wanted to tell you earlier, but didn't have a chance—"

"Tell me what?"

"That Mr. Fortescue from the university is here. Downstairs. With your father."

"Laurence is here? Right now?" Hetty's hand went to her hair immediately to check how she looked. Her heart in her throat, she flung the blankets back.

"Miss, you can't go down there like this."

"Then help me ready myself."

"Beg your pardon, Miss, but your brother told me to be sure you stayed in that bed and ate your dinner."

"But you're my maid. You must do as I say."

Mary didn't have to respond to that as John returned at that moment.

"I heard what you said and under no circumstances are you to go down there. Their conversation has nothing to do with you." He looked at Hetty slyly. "And besides, didn't you tell me a few minutes ago that you're not interested in the man?"

"He's a caller, that's all. I should be down there to help Father entertain."

"You're in no condition to go downstairs. Doctor Waverly will be here any moment."

"Did someone say my name?" An elderly man with a shock of white hair and bushy mustache came in the room.

Hetty let out a deep sigh. Now she would never get to see Laurence.

End of excerpt *Lightning Strikes Twice* (The Heart of a Hero Series) by Jillian Chantal

Chapter One Excerpt from:

No Hiding for the Guilty
The Heart of a Hero Series

Copyright © 2017 Vanessa Riley

Chapter One

July 1813 Devonshire, England

THE VELVET FOG engulfed Isadel Armijo, swallowing her whole like a lump of brown bread drowning in white soup. She flinched at a noise from behind. She pulled on the reins of her stolen horse and swiveled in the saddle to see if she was followed.

Nothing.

Nothing but night was behind her. And nothing would be for her if she didn't keep moving. Bundled up in Papa's old coat and breeches, she was still just a female alone, but one on the greatest adventure. One of honor. Well, that's what she told herself when she snuck away from Hartland Abbey.

She kicked her mount forward. The thick fog closed in. Isadel couldn't see, couldn't breathe, couldn't feel anything but heaviness as if she'd be dragged down at any moment. She swatted the air with her straw hat as she had from the boat deck the eve she emigrated from Spain. The half-done thing had been scooped up from a blocking tool of a neighbor's burnt out workshop. The lady spy had slapped it upon Isadel's head as they fled Badajoz.

If Isadel closed her eyes and thought hard of that night, she'd smell the soot that consumed her city. If there was a God, then he should let black powder smell the same. Then, this hat would be a crown ordaining her destiny.

A branch slapped her cheek. The horse must've veered left and into the woods. Fear swept through her. What if this wasn't the way to Bannerman, but to another of Lord Wellington's spies? None of them had the skills she needed. Bannerman was the one, the only one up to the task and the only one who hated her enemy as much as Isadel.

Clinging closer to the horse's neck, she had to trust the beast knew the way. Trust—the word made her raw nerves snap like uncooked fidelli noodles, but this past year, she learned that her employer, Lord Hartland, was friended by men of precision, those set to provide justice. Who else needed justice more than Isadel? Who else had lost as much?

Her mottled colored mount whinnied but kept moving forward into the thickets. The night had grown dark again. She could barely see and hoped this gelding could navigate its way like the boat captain that spy woman, Joanna Pearson, had bribed. The captain slipped through the low salty clouds of the Bay of Biscay as if he possessed an inner compass guiding him toward the North Star. Isadel understood, for her inner compass aimed solely at vengeance.

The animal lurched then started to the right again. She stilled her fingers on the smooth leather strap of its rein. Humming her mother's tune, the one that timed her whisking strokes to perfection, didn't distract the horse. It began moving faster down a steep incline. When they reached the bottom, the clouds parted. She could see again and witnessed moonlight kissing the white stones lining the trail. It was the first light she'd seen since leaving Lord Hartland's Abbey at sundown.

When the housekeeper discovered her missing, the old battle-ax would screech that "the half-breed" done run off. This time the old woman's fear of Isadel's kind being evil or a thief would be true.

Stomach souring, she slapped the reins between her palms. These hands were meant for making pastries, forming biscuits, for stirring delicate sauces, not unlocking doors and unfurling the stocks keeping a horse stabled. Yet, her fingertips had grown tired of wiping midnight tears. If she did nothing, her gift of pastries and breads would feed her enemy, the man who had destroyed her world. Moldona would come to the Abbey at month's end.

Deflating in her saddle like a cake that fell from too much checking, she threw her arms tighter around her mount's neck and clung to it as if it were her father. With a breath, gulping in the strong sweaty horse's lather, she sat up straight and dared her eyes to grow wet. A woman destined to kill shouldn't be weepy. That was a victim's plight, and she refused to wear that crown anymore. Her greatest wish must come true. She'd risked everything to make things right, her spotless reputation and her safe employment from a man who made sure his staff treated her fairly. The earl's disappointment in her character would kill her faster than the lashings he could demand to punish a horse thief. If he exercised his rights like the wealthy hacienda owners in Spain, he'd ask for a hanging.

Too late to turn back, not that she wanted to, she kept on, urging the horse saying, "To Bann-er-man, horse. To Bann-er-man."

Another hour of hard riding and the smell of the sea, fresh and salty, seemed stronger. Soon, she should be able to see Sandon Manor, the castle hiding the reclusive spy. Fingers vibrating, she swiped at her mouth dabbing at the fresh blood coming from the corner. She'd bit down with the last jostle of the horse. How horrid she must look, probably seeming more like a lost urchin than a cook. She couldn't wear her neat uniform and keep her seat, and who needed to fret about getting creases upon her starched apron while stealing away? Riding like a man, in men's breeches just looked easy. It wasn't. It was quite hard for someone with short legs. Papa would say she was barely enough stones in weight to fill a messenger's saddlebag.

Patting the horse, she gave him a moment to catch his breath. She needed to let her pulse slow and leaned back, gazing at the rocky incline ahead of her. The slope stretched high, sticking into the clouds headless as if it had been axed like a roasting chicken. Her stomach rumbled and all she could think of was how odd it was now to remember being hungry. Did they feed prisoners in English jails? Maybe they'd shoot first and ask questions later like the British soldiers had done at Badajoz.

Righteous anger welled inside her growling gut, but so did a little teaspoon of hope. With a click of her heels, she urged the gelding forward. If the horse had done its job, she'd see Sandon from the top. Then she'd know that she'd stolen the right horse, that she'd come to the right place. She'd have a chance to no longer live with hate. "Go to Bann-er-man."

Gravel flew on every side. Isadel became breathless. The final push through the fog made her heart flip against her ribs and stay there. The pounding in her chest hurt so badly her ribs would surely poke through her coarse nankeen shirt. Papa's shirt. Bracing in the saddle, Isadel held on as her mount leapt above the clouds to the top, a flat plateau covering the hill.

Quiet surrounded her and she tugged at the strap, stopping the horse. The air smelled clean and sweet, like after the rain or a good cleaning. The salt, it burned her nostrils, only because she breathed so hard. Yet maybe it cleansed. If there was a heaven, this had to be it—quiet, pure, sweet—unseeing of the horrors below, untouched by the death of innocence—the scream of a sister, the unanswered begging prayer of Papa.

Clouds swirled for a moment, then opened and showed things—tree groves, the waters of the Bristol Channel. Joy leaped inside. They'd made it to the coast. Sandon had to be near. The tired part of her wanted to linger in this peace, but to stay in heaven was to deny the hell she'd lived. Morning meant discovery of her theft, no new mercies, no more chances. She steered the horse to the edge. The wind picked up again, spreading the fog, making it thin in spots. The gaps appeared like the insides of white Emmental cheese.

With wide eyes, she beheld the sight she'd seen from the boat smuggling her to these shores, the high turret of Sandon Manor. It was again alone in the night sky just as it had been nine months ago. With her finger, she traced the structure down to the rest of the castle, which lay shrouded by trees. The turret looked daunting, almost whispering, "don't reach for me," but Isadel had to. She stood in the stirrups and became deaf to the warning. She risked too much to turn back now. Bannerman had to see her. He had to help.

With a gulp, she hunkered down and pressed forward. The horse flew down the hill, galloping faster, sinking deeper into the steamy fog. They moved as one, splashing through mud puddles. She blocked low branches with her hand and ducked under tree limbs. The horse knew the path, slipping through openings that didn't seem to exist. It trotted, weaving and threading through the dense blanket of leaves. The horse stopped on the castle's rock-strewn drive.

Isadel sized up the worn door, the overgrowth of vines hugging the limestone brick. That sense of being alone, of not wanting to bear the company of others, closed in upon her, but she welcomed it and pushed it into her heart. Nothing alleviated her misery more than the isolation of not explaining, of not searching for ways to fit into this very English world. Emboldened, she jumped down and walked with her chin up to the door.

It took three knocks, three shifts in her stance, three stampings of her short boots, before the door opened. A grizzled man with a lantern and a balding head glared at her. "We've no use for beggars, boy."

Boy? She surely must look like one with her hair pulled up in her hat. Yet, being thought a man might serve her. "Sir." She coughed and deepened her hoarse voice. "I'm no beggar. I'm a cook...chef."

"Don't need one of those either."

A thief and want-to-be-murderer had no room for shame. Shoving all the pride she had left into her spine, she stood up straight, probably exposing her ankles from her father's old breeches. He wasn't that tall either. "I bring a message for your employer, Bann-er-man."

The man wriggled his hooked nose. "Jump on your horse and leave, cook-chef. Take it with you."

She curled her tongue and tried that long name again in what she hoped sounded clipped, very English. "I'm here for Mr. Bannerman." She kept her voice even making sure no hitch of feminine desperation could be heard. "It's a matter of death."

Brow furrowing with more crevices, the fellow pulled a knife from his pocket, waving it as if to intimidate her, but she'd skinned too many chickens for that. "So you're looking for him? You'll have to kill me to get to him."

Kill this man? He needed to know her private thoughts of murder had nothing to do with his master, well not really. She raised her hands and shook her head. "Not here for that."

"Then what, boy? Why did you come?"

Like Papa, she spread her feet apart and tried to seem rooted and certain. "Your master is safe from me. And he'll see me. I come from Lord Hartland." She let her gaze lift to the grand stairs behind the gatekeeper. "Is Bannerman in the tower? I can run up there and deliver the message."

Happy her tone sounded clear, she pushed inside, but the old fellow stepped in her path.

"I said no visitors."

She was too close to lose out now. Fumbling with Papa's coat, she produced the letter and fluttered it, exposing the earl's wax mark. "Tell the master that I have a letter from Hartland. He has to see this."

He held out his palm, but there was no way Isadel would give him the letter. She couldn't, not without an audience with the explosives expert. "I must only offer this to Bannerman."

After sixty beats of her heart, the man nodded his thin pointy chin and waved her further inside. "You don't look like an assassin."

Assassin? Isadel wanted to be one, just not for Bannerman. "I'm a messenger, today."

"Scrawny you? Yes, that's what Hartland would send. No turret for you, boy. The drawing room. Easier for you to make your delivery then go."

So, Bannerman was up there. Did he enjoy the air, the hazy night sky, that feeling of being on top of the world?

Before her longing for peace drove her up those stairs, she focused on the old man and traipsed behind him. Trying hard not to stare at the holes in the wall or the torn tapestries, she focused on what to say to Bannerman. Yet, the melon-sized holes, the broken lath and plaster sent a tremor to her middle. What could have done it? Who would dare destroy the gilded trim, the papered orange walls? This place was nothing like the duke's beautiful Abbey.

The butler turned to her, and she dropped her gaze. She wasn't here to assess the housekeeping. This destruction was none of her business.

The fellow stopped at a door half-off its hinges. He pressed it open and waved her inside. "Wait in here. Make sure the brass doorknobs and books remain."

Without protest, Isadel nodded. What the old man thought of her meant nothing, just like the insults of her employer's staff. Talk was cheap, and it couldn't kill a soul that had already died from sorrow. Every hope she ever possessed went away with her father and sister's murder at the hands of British pigs. The only thing worth anything to Isadel was revenge.

The door shut behind her with a thud. How it managed to stay upright was a wonder. The room was cold and grey. A fire seemed to be dying. Someone had left it to wither. Bannerman? He couldn't be in the turret and here, too. Maybe the rumors of him dying and becoming a ghost were true, but then why would Lord Hartland keep sending him notes?

She rubbed at her forehead. A hint of oak and tobacco hit her nose as she walked closer to the desk. The one time she made Bannerman tea, he had sat in Hartland's library with a pile of books about ancient medicine at his feet as he puffed on a pipe. Reading seemed to ease his restlessness.

Her skin prickled as she took another deep inhale and prepared to see the big hulk of a man again. The right words to get him to agree to return to the Abbey Estate and help her kill her enemy hadn't materialized.

Her stomach soured, rolling in her famished middle. She hadn't thought this part out enough. Pacing from the large patio door to a book-laden desk, she tried to number her arguments. She stopped and fingered an open tome upon the smooth maple writing surface. A recipe for skin lotion made with arsenic dotted the page. That's not very good. Papa had warned her and her sister about the horrible practices women used to lighten their skin.

With a shake of her head, she stepped back, then loosened a button of her bulky jacket and fanned her head with her hat. Her nerves had her heart racing again. She shoved the hat back on, scooping up a thick curl that had come loose. Her resolve of not caring what she looked like, or even that she favored a boy, began to slip. She would see the fastidious Bannerman again as a wrinkled frog.

Maybe like a genie or a handsome prince, he'd grant her wish. She didn't need a kiss to break a curse, but craved a black powder recipe, which would make beastly Moldona disappear.

The door behind her blew open, rattling pages from the rush of air. The shock of it hitting the wall made her duck as if avoiding gunshot or a cannon's fire. She bit her lip and spun. A huge man barreled toward her. "Bannerman?"

"Yes. It's good to know the name of the man who will kill you."

Dark gold, almost red hair covered his face like thick lion fur. The wavy locks that had been parted to perfection were gone, replaced by wild curls. He looked like a beast, a large, hulking beast.

She stepped toward the door, but he flung a poker in her direction. It whizzed past her head, missing her temple by an inch. With a thunk, it sunk into the wall. "I didn't say you could go."

A gasp left her, but then she caught his hazel eyes, the ones she'd spied at the Abbey Estate, the ones that lit in laughter to Lord Hartland's jests. Wellington's explosives expert stood in front of her. "Bannerman, sir, it is you."

He swiped at his mane. "How dare Hartland send someone for me again. I'm done."

Stomping toward his desk, he kicked an emerald chair, sending it sliding across the scarred mahogany floor. It stopped an inch from her boot, but she stood still and stared at him.

As if filled with remorse, he rubbed a gloved hand over his face then pivoted toward the hearth. "Boy, what favor does he want? Or does he send news? Has he found the Almeida Killer?"

More confused at the changes in the once well-groomed man she'd seen a few months ago than by his gibberish about Almeida, she pitched her head side to side. "I'm not sure if his note has more news of a two-year old bloodbath that savaged my Spanish lands. But, I know he wants you to return with me."

"No! Hart will not order me around. Nor will one of his foot soldiers."

His voice felt like thunder. His shaking fist would surely hit with a punch of lightning, still she held the note out to him.

"I swore to him I'd kill the next messenger who came to me." Bannerman flexed his gloved fingers. "I guess you're the lucky one he chose to die."

Death didn't scare Isadel any more than living with regrets. She folded her arms about her. "I've always been lucky like that."

"I'll give it to Hartland. He knew how much the former me liked a good joke. But a dead man has no room for laughter or more guilt. Return to Hart and tell him no."

She stamped her foot like a girl, but hardened her voice. "Do your worst, or return with me to Hartland Abbey. No middle ground."

He came near. She could smell the stench of metal coming from his arm or his hand—so like her father's apothecary shop. His arms flexed as he hovered. He was large, larger than she remembered, but as a good servant, she'd never been this near to him.

His scent, ferrous or sulfur, strangled. "No one gives me ultimatums."

If this was the end, part of her was glad of it. Straightening her spine, she held her breath and waited to be throttled, waited for darkness to overcome her when he choked the air from her throat betwixt his large hands. That had to be a better fate than going to prison or living with the knowledge she'd failed at her one chance to kill her enemy.

Hugh Bannerman raised his hands ready to punch the messenger through the wall as he'd done with everyone else who'd stood against him, but the boy merely did the task Hart had requested, just as Phipps, his man-of-all-work would do. Hugh took a breath and lowered his fists. He turned and let his frustration meet the desk. When he tapped it, the legs split and sent his piles of research spilling to the floor.

He flexed his palm, but the rapid action hadn't caused his hand to bleed again. Relieved, he pivoted but frowned to mask his concern and said, "So you are prepared to die, boy? Or is Hart prepared to let you die? Must be tough knowing how expendable your life is?"

The foolhardy messenger shrugged. "I sent myself. Didn't know there were extra benefits for coming."

Hugh almost laughed. The boy wasn't frightened, maybe he even had a death wish like himself. Hart was a better spy for he probably prepared the boy. Maybe even told the lad of Hugh's vow to never take another life. Never again would he willingly take an innocent spirit, even of his enemies. He'd be a man of principle like his brother.

"Hartland says the situation is dire."

"It's always dire. I have retired. I'll be merciful and give you one last chance to leave. Mercy is a good thing for an active spy to possess." Hugh rubbed his stubbly beard. The dry skin beneath itched worse with each treatment. "Pity, I'm retired. And volunteering is a dangerous business. Why did you elect yourself?"

The sorry fellow in baggy breeches that hit the floor bent his head. "I need... Lord Hartland needs you to return."

His voice sounded light and weak, maybe even feminine. "So, Hart's running out of men. You're barely breeched. What are you like seven?"

The slight fellow tossed the note on the floor at Hugh's boot. "Old enough, and I wanted to see the man he brags on, the one who killed hundreds, even people standing beside him with his detonations and nary a scratch happened to his person."

At least this boy had guts to utter such nonsense. Perhaps this gall is how he slipped past Phipps. "There's always a scratch. Some just can't be seen."

He turned and struck a stinking sulfurous match and lit candles on the mantle. Pivoting back, he pointed to the paper. "Why don't you pick that up, and we'll start this again?"

The messenger put a shaking hand to his hip. "With the threats or without?"

So, the fellow was nervous. Good. He thought about forcing him to scoop up the letter, but the runt would probably freeze like a scared rabbit or vomit all over himself like the last two grooms. Hugh relented, bent and picked up Hart's impressive parchment folded with perfect crisp line. "I'll have to keep my option to kill you open, you know. Especially since you're making me work."

A hint of cloves or maybe cinnamon wafted from the paper. Very odd for Hart. He started to open the letter then stopped. It would be no different than the last summons. Something was in crisis that needed his explosion making skills or maybe, just maybe he'd figured out the identity of the Almeida Killer and sent a warning. Hart was a good man, even to his gruff friends. "The world didn't end with my rejection of your master's last two requests. I'm sure it won't with this one."

Staring as if he could see through Hugh, the boy's eyes, a cross between henna and gold grew wider. "But you must return. There will be no hope for me if you don't."

Bannerman closed his gloved fingers about the paper. Had he left some bit of greying skin exposed? Maybe he hadn't been careful and the messenger saw his strange leprosy. "Did anyone ever tell you it was impolite to gawk?"

"You kicked a chair at me, sir. Perhaps that makes things even."

Stuffing his one hand behind his back, Hugh leaned against the hearth, and looked away from the young man and the shadows consuming the dim room. Sandon wasn't always like this. "Be gone. I don't make idle threats."

Waiting for the boy to wilt and blow away, Hugh let his gaze drift into the flames. In the smoke and flying ash, he saw the face of another young man, one with a quick wit who talked for days about what he would do with Sandon once their father relented and allowed him to manage it separate their stepmother's influence. Then Henry would wax on about the missionary trip he would take. Grandeur and respectability—that was the Bannerman family bond.

Both the living and the dead would hate how Hugh allowed the place to fester like the plague rotting his skin. He whipped his palm near the flames reaching for the missing poker, remembering too late that he'd sent it crashing into the wall. He pivoted and eased his arms to the side. "You're still here? You came to die?"

The fellow looked placid, too calm. "I have a death wish. That is why I am here."

The letter in Bannerman's fingers seemed less important. Curiosity about the messenger and his boldness took control. He had a kinship to the absurd, something he'd forsaken for too long, not since his brother. With a grunt, he dropped the letter to the scratched surface of his desk. "You didn't just come to drop off Lord Hartland's note? Out with it."

Pulling at his loose collar and baggy jacket, the fellow shifted his stance. "You are right. I came for me. Lord Hartland doesn't know that I am the one delivering this correspondence."

Hugh groaned loud and long. "Let me guess. You need revenge. I've injured someone in your family. A drunken row? Or better, I killed some traitor in your blood..." He paused for a second, his eyes for the first time taking notice of the footman's off colored skin, the thicker full lips. "Well, one of your bloodlines. A traitor who dares to be against Mother England. What are you, Spanish? From Almeida?"

When the boy shifted his stance, Hugh readied to pounce. The Almeida Killer had already killed three of his fellow commanders of that siege. Soon, the only living English soldiers remaining would be Hugh, Nev, Moldona, Cox and Wellesley. "Take care your next action. It could be your last."

The boy shuffled his lean fingers, ones surely too delicate to maim a living soul, over his mouth. He wiped off beads of sweat. Then he stopped and shoved his nervous palms to his backside. "I want revenge, but not against you. I need you to teach me how to make an explosion, one deadly controlled explosion. I only need to kill one man."

As if he had held his breath, the boy let it out in a huff then shrugged his shoulders.

Foolish mortal. If Hugh could find humor from the misguided fool, it might give ease to his nerves tonight allowing more time for the latest lesions on his hands to heal. "Killing someone sounds easy, very righteous in the planning, but things rarely work as intended. Consequences follow even when things don't work."

"This one has to work. I don't want others hurt, just Moldona."

The room seemed to close in upon Hugh. Luckily, his practice of subterfuge kept him upright. Moldona wasn't his rival anymore, just the man who'd stolen Betsy, the love of Hugh's life away. "So, you want to murder the Conqueror of Badajoz?"

"I'm from Badajoz. You hate him. Lord Hartland said you did." The messenger stepped closer. Desperation painted his long lean face. "I need your help."

"Everyone is from somewhere. That doesn't make you special. Go back to Hartland. Tell him no. I'm not returning."

"I can't go back." He bent and pulled a knife from his boot and tossed it at Hugh's foot. "Kill me as you said. I'm a horse thief. As Lord Hartland's friend, it is in your right."

The amusement drained away as he stared at the shiny blade. It wasn't the type you'd have to fend off a footpad, but something he'd seen in a kitchen. He picked it up. "Boy, do you know who I am? I don't kill like this."

"I know who you are. I came because of that. And I'd rather die here than a little everyday with my memories." The fellow spun and ran. His footfalls didn't sound as if he'd fled toward the house door but deeper into Sandon. The boy said he was a thief. What could he possibly steal from here?

"Bannerman!"

His man's yell told Hugh he'd soon find out.

Rushing out of the drawing room, he saw old Phipps running from the stairs. His face was blood red like when he discovered a new hole in the wall, or something else Hugh had broken.

"Lord Hartland's groom. He's in the turret. I think he's going to jump."

Suicide was a coward's death. His admiration for the messenger died.

Bannerman turned and put his fingers on the shaft of the family sword, Henry's sword, but pulled away as if he'd touched flames. He didn't think himself worthy to finger the prized possession only to scare off a coward. Instead, he'd use his fists and readied to smash sense into the fool. He pushed past Phipps and pounded to the stairs, taking them by twos. The old structure creaked, surely his weight would make them break and fall apart on his next fevered rant.

When he reached the turret, he found the boy sitting on the broken sill with legs dangling in the night air.

He truly would jump and that set Hugh's heart pumping like it did when he struck a match to a detonation cord. It would only be a few more seconds before the blast and the smell of death claimed the air. "Boy, it doesn't have to be this way. You are living on your hate. You think it goes away when you die?"

The messenger didn't turn, but kept facing straight ahead pointed toward the sky. "The air does feel cold here. If the fog weren't so greedy, you could see for miles, maybe even eternity. The air feels cold like God's breath. If I squint, maybe I can see him stir the waters."

Pounding closer, Hugh came near enough that he could grab the lad or assist him in leaping. It was too soon to test his vow of never killing. One more footfall, a few more seconds, that's what Hugh needed to make a difference. "So, what's your name?"

"You didn't care before." The gravel in the boy's voice became less, but it held no tears. It sounded of raw anger. "Don't pretend now."

"Boy. I'm a spy. That is what we do, but this is crazy. And why stain my walls? Old Phipps and I will have to clean up your bones from the garden."

Still not turning, he let go of the sill with one hand and cupped his eyes. "That will be a hardship since cleaning is something you are not apt to do." He sighed. "Those soft clouds. The rush of the wind, so peaceful and endless... You think this is what freedom truly looks like?"

The wobbly window started to crack. It moaned like it would break. Hugh had kicked it in his last crazed fever. Well, he punished it and every spare wall in Sandon. Now close enough to grab the boy, Hugh could stop the suicide, but a man needed a chance to choose. Another day, he'd give into weakness again, for those demons of depression pressed late into the night, even at Hugh. He leaned over and grabbed the upper edge of the open window. "You have too much humor inside to jump. Come inside and convince me of why I should help you kill Moldona."

"You just don't want to clean." The boy leaned forward and kicked his boots like he was at the water's edge. "Tell me why it's best to see a tomorrow with no justice."

Above the peaceful wind noise, the fool's voice sounded as if it bore pain. The boy was too young for that. He didn't know the frustration of guessing how to tamp down his own strength or how to stop wearing upon his skin the guilt of every death he'd caused. No that was Hugh's special torment. "You don't know anything. You are young and alive. Everything seems tragic."

Hugh reached out and grasped his shoulder. "This ends now."

The boy's hat flew away as they struggled.

Hugh's fingers tore off the jacket and pieces of his shirt, revealing a corset and curves. He'd uncovered a lass. "What? You came to trick me?"

Raven hair spilled down her back as she turned. With her hands, she covered her chemise and tottered on the open sill. The wood gave way. She fell forward, but he caught an arm. "Woman."

He refused to let go as they both dangled out of the window.

End of excerpt *No Hiding for the Guilty* (The Heart of a Hero Series) by Vanessa Riley

Chapter One Excerpt from:

The Marquis of Thunder
The Heart of a Hero Series

Chapter One

April, 1813
Nottinghamshire, England

THE SKIES WERE seething with dark clouds. Distant thunder rolled over the surrounding hillsides, ominous in its persistence. The storm would be raging soon; it would show no deference for Lord Thorston, the infamous Marquis of Thunder.

Indeed, Thorston was about to get wet. He felt it in his bones.

His horse felt it, too. The elegant black shuddered with nervous energy. Thorston patted him for reassurance.

"We'll be there soon, long before the first drops, my friend."

His mount flicked his ears and tossed his dark head. For a truth, it wasn't raindrops the sleek thoroughbred feared, it was his namesake. Five years ago, when Thorston had named the colt, he'd thought he was simply paying homage to his own unfortunate epithet. At the time he had no idea he was being ironically prophetic. Thunder, unfortunately, was terrified of thunder.

Thorston knew he had better get them both safely to Northgate Hall before the storm hit. He barely held his worried animal under control as it was. If they were out here much longer, Thunder was likely to go into a panic. Thorston touched his mount's sides and gently urged him into a trot.

Rounding a sharp curve in the road, he was forced to pull up to a stop. Thunder champed and snorted as a too-near flash of lightning cut through the clouds. The corresponding thunder answered a few short seconds later. Progress, however, was impossible.

The roadway ahead seemed to be blocked by a flock of jostling sheep. One very determined collie dog darted about, keeping the flock tightly together, perfectly in the way. Thunder shied backward and Thorston calmed him as best he could, searching the steep banks on each side of the road for a possible escape.

The ancient roadway had been worn deep into the landscape. The earth rose up on either side, with decaying rock walls lining the rim above that. Tufts of grass spilled over the edge. There was no chance of getting a horse up out of the roadway here.

He could not reach Northgate Hall as he'd hoped. At this point, he'd be lucky to reach the village that lay between them and the ancient estate. But to get even as far as Lesser Crossing he still had to get past these damnable sheep.

Apparently he would have to convince Thunder to backtrack. They'd have to ride toward the storm for half a mile or so before they might find a way up, out of the rut and over the wall. And then they'd have to negotiate the soggy fields. The road they traveled on ran roughly parallel to the River Trent. This storm was not the first to pass through in recent days and the river was already breaching its banks. The road was treacherous enough.

Sending Thunder through open grazing lands would not make for quick headway.

It seemed there was no other route. He was about to turn the animal to retrace their steps when his eye caught on something. A lone figure appeared, rising up from a stooped position in the midst of the sheep. Not one of the local farmers as Thorston might have expected, but a woman. Instantly he worried that she was in danger, trapped by the agitated animals and likely to be trampled.

To his surprise, though, she whistled at the dog who immediately came to her aid and directed the sheep away from her. Unflustered, she stooped down again. Thorston sat up higher in his saddle to see what might have her attention in such a tenuous situation. He could not tell, so he nudged Thunder to move closer.

The horse was unsure, but trusted Thorston's leading and took a few hesitant steps. The dog glanced their way, but seemed to care only for the sheep. They pushed and pressed against each other, their noisy feet and worried cries only slightly louder than the gathering wind and distant thunder.

The woman, Thorston could see now, was down low in the gap through the bank at the right side of the road. Apparently this was an area that was used as a crossing. The rock wall that lined the roadway was obviously a barrier that usually kept the sheep out of the road. Now, as the river on one side was rising the sheep needed to be moved to pasture on the other side. Something was blocking their passage. A gate, from what Thorston could see. It should be open, but it was not.

Why this lone woman was out here trying to repair it by herself, he had no idea. He could see easily, though, that she could use some help. Whatever obstacle she struggled with seemed to be more than she could handle.

Thorston slid off Thunder and prayed the horse wouldn't spook and bolt away. There was no telling how far the terrified animal would run without Thorston's governance. It was risky to leave him in the road now, but the pitiful sight of the woman—a young one, at that—struggling at the rock wall in the midst of all those nervous sheep was not something he could turn his back on.

If Fate had granted him anything, it was strong arms and a broad back. His tailor often complained of his less-than-elegant musculature and his own father chastised him for participating in frequent strenuous exercise unbefitting a gentleman. Thorston ignored them both, of course. His physique and his experience made him perfectly qualified to render assistance in this moment, and by God he would do so.

He only hoped it would be in time to avoid the tempest that blustered and swirled in the wall of dark clouds that roiled steadily toward them. Despite his broad back and generous stature, Thorston had no great desire to be drenched today. The unpleasant nature of his visit to this area was more than enough to have put him in a sour mood. The sooner he could get the young woman and her sheep out of his way, the sooner he could get himself and his horse to safety, then get on with his business.

Seraphina steadied her foot on the large, moss-covered rock and steeled herself for another try. The wind carried the scent of rain and the current of urgency. Any moment now the heavens would open and unleash their downpour. She had to get this gate open and drive the sheep up to higher ground.

Unfortunately, the rocks had tumbled, trapping the heavy wooden timbers that ordinarily would have been removable to allow passage. Unless she could miraculously shift the rocks, the whole lot of them would be trapped in this narrow gully as the river raged higher and higher over its banks. She knew this area flooded often and it had not been her intent to leave the sheep in the low pastures at this time of year.

But secrets had to be kept, so here she was tackling the problem long after she should have and totally alone. Papa's health had required her extra attention these last days, and she'd been especially mindful of that more than anything. He did not need to learn about things that might upset him. Such as a flock of sheep that had not been listed among their assets when she and their man of business tabulated their rents.

Ordinarily Seraphina would be opposed to any sort of deception, but Papa was so fragile, and their man of business assured her that this was the only way to make ends meet. Papa needed to feel calm and secure, he needed his physician and medicines, and Seraphina needed to do whatever it took to see that he got those things.

Surely the duke would not suffer if the rents he received from them were slightly less than usual. They had heard nothing from the man in years. She wondered if he would even notice if they did not bother to send the rent money at all.

But of course that would be dangerous, and this was not the time to court danger. With all that was going on—the war on the Continent, the war in America, the violence and unrest here between workers and mill owners—it was hardly the time to do anything but try to survive.

And that was getting harder every day. Papa's last two hired men had now come up missing—gone with no word and no warning. The household staff was down to a bare minimum, and Papa's meager investments had failed. If they lost the flock to flash flooding, it would send them into ruin. She'd already sold the wool—even though it was still on the sheep—to one of the local hosiers. How could she ever pay him back if they did not have the wool to give him?

But because they did not officially have these sheep, she couldn't very well go around begging for help with them. She really had made a fine mess for herself and now here she was, surrounded by animals much heavier than she while a raging storm bore down on them all. She had no one to turn to, just her own strength and Tess, her tireless sheepdog who was doing her best to keep the sheep under control even as a bright flash of lightning sizzled the air all around them.

The sudden shriek of a horse accompanied the flash, just moments before a loud boom of thunder rattled the earth. Seraphina jumped. The dog darted across the road to keep the sheep from erupting into mindless frenzy, but as the thunder rolled over the landscape the frantic effort seemed pointless. The sheep would rush back over the other bank and be trapped in the lower meadow, easy prey for the gluttonous river. As soon as this next downpour was unleashed, flooding would be inevitable and swift.

It appeared the only thing keeping the sheep from breaking past Tess now was the huge black horse that seemed to appear out of nowhere. He stood in the narrow road just slightly above them, his rider completely composed despite the tenuous situation. Seraphina shoved her damp, disheveled hair out of her face so she could get a better look. Had someone come to help her? One of the men from their village, perhaps?

No, the man on the horse was no one she'd ever seen before. No one from Lesser Crossing had ever cut such a fine—and enormous—figure. The stranger sat tall and straight on his stately mount, apparently impervious to the weather. The horse danced nervously, but the man kept him expertly in check. Even his hat sat obediently atop his head in elegant perfection, defying the wind. The man's cloak was as black as the horse and the multiple capes flapped like foreboding wings behind him.

Seraphina could not make out his features, but one distinguishing element caught her eye. The man, although clad in black on the huge midnight steed, was not a dark figure. It surprised her to note that beneath his raven top hat, he was crowned with a shock of wild, waving hair that was every bit as yellow as her own. It was almost as if some golden archangel had donned human attire and dropped from the heavens, assuming gentlemanly form.

Unfortunately, at this moment she didn't need an archangel or a gentleman. She needed someone who knew something about dislodging big rocks and keeping sheep from drowning. In her limited experience, she'd never found angels nor gentlemen to be particularly useful in either of these.

Apparently he was willing to give it a go. The man dismounted, his horse becoming noticeably more nervous with his absence. Seraphina half expected the animal to charge off in the other direction when the man dropped the reins and took a step toward her. It didn't bolt, which she counted as a testament to the man's horsemanship, or perhaps his ability to install dread in anyone who might wish to disregard his will.

"Are you having some trouble there?" he called. His voice boomed over the gusting wind and bleating sheep.

"I need to get the sheep into higher pasture," she yelled, hoping her own voice might somehow carry. "But I can't move the bar that is blocking our way. It's wedged under these rocks."

He must have understood because he glanced toward the low-lying meadow that the sheep had been in and nodded. Her collie growled as the man advanced toward them. Seraphina murmured an admonition.

"Easy, Tess. I'll let you know when it's time to bite the fellow."

Tess dropped low to the ground, ears back, her gaze flicking warily between the man and sheep under her command. Seraphina had no doubt in her faithful canine. One motion from her—the slightest whistle—and Tess would forget herding duty and become a formidable protector. But how effective could it be against such a man?

His clothes and his voice gave the appearance of social standing, but his broad shoulders and strong stride hinted at a more physical power. The man was huge, and built as a laborer. Surely if he were so inclined, he just might be able to do something constructive for them. If he were not so inclined, however, Seraphina could be in for some trouble.

She was not quite sure what his inclinations were right now.

"A sturdy hammer might be useful for this," he said, uncomfortably near.

"It would," she agreed, standing as tall as she could and keeping eye contact with Tess. "But my hammer got caught when those rocks tumbled, pinning it as well as the bar that I need to move."

He leaned in, so close to her she could smell the scent of his soap. His shoulders practically blocked the light and his very nearness took her breath away. Before she could react to defend herself, he was reaching, stooping so that his face was almost against hers. She choked on her surprise, but as quickly as his action terrified her she realized what he was doing.

He had his hand on the shank of the hammer where it stuck out from under the pile. If she'd been in control of her tongue she would have reminded him that it was pointless, that she'd already tried—and failed—to remove it. When the rocks in the wall had tumbled, they'd trapped it securely. His attempt would be fruitless.

But she couldn't tell him that. The words simply wouldn't form as her eyes caught on his, locked in an uncomfortable but unbreakable union. In the icy blue depths she saw defiance, impatience, assurance, and perhaps even a touch of mirth. Was he enjoying his needless display of supposed superiority? Yes. The hint of a smile at the corner of his lip gave him away. He stared at her with the most annoying overconfidence.

Soon it would be her turn to smile when he tried to retrieve the hammer and found that, indeed, it was stuck. She smiled her own hint of a smile to imagine such a proud gentleman humiliated by a simple workman's tool. He would not be so smug then, would he?

Her imagining was short lived, though. The hammer, it seemed, was even more intimidated by him than she was. It didn't so much as try to frustrate his arrogance. With one effortless tug, the hulking stranger pulled the traitorous implement free of the rocks.

The hammer was his and he held it up before her. Lightning flashed through the darkening clouds. The man's golden hair tossed in waves with the wind. Thunder rumbled with the same timbre as his voice.

He grinned when he spoke. "I'm good with hammers. Now, how can I help you, little shepherdess?"

End of excerpt *The Marquis of Thunder* (The Heart of a Hero Series) by Susan Gee Heino

Chapter One Excerpt from:

The Good, The Bad, And The Scandalous
The Heart of a Hero Series

Chapter One

London, August 1812

SARAH SHIPTON HALTED on the stairs to the offices above the bookshop her parents—correction, her *mother*—owned. She could hear the sound of quiet weeping, yet the sun had barely cleared the horizon and no one was due in for at least another hour. She tiptoed up the rest of the stairs with her skirts clutched in one hand, pausing at the top to listen again, forgetting all about the odd man who had followed her for half of her walk to the shop.

"Oh, Thomas..."

The voice belonged to her mother and a flash of understanding lit Sarah's mind. Her father had died six months ago and though Mrs. Shipton had calmly taken the reins of their business, she was still occasionally overcome by grief.

Sarah snuck down to the bottom of the stairs then once again made her way to the landing, this time with heavy footsteps. By the time she entered the clerk's room where her mother was sitting, Mrs. Shipton had wiped her tears away and blown her nose. Her eyes were still red and swollen, but Sarah pretended not to notice.

"Mother! I didn't expect to see you here so early this morning." Sarah kept her tone light and hoped she sounded surprised.

Mrs. Shipton smiled at her daughter. "I didn't expect to see you here, either. I thought for sure you'd be sleeping in today after arriving home so late last night."

Sarah's mouth curved into a smile of her own. She'd spent the past month visiting her aunt and cousins in Dover, enjoying the summer sun...and the company of the local squire's steward.

"You know I'm no good at lying about all day. I thought I would go over the accounts this morning, then help Mr. Higgins with the new inventory."

"Oh." Mrs. Shipton's face crumpled and Sarah watched her mother struggle for several painful moments to bring her emotions under control. "I don't know how to say this, but...there is no new inventory."

"Nothing new today?" That was odd. There was always something coming into the shop—second printings of popular books, the newest Minerva Press novel, special orders for customers who wanted something particular.

"Nothing new at all."

"Why not?"

Mrs. Shipton reached out and took her daughter's hand as tears dripped down her cheeks again. "The bookshop has been losing money for months. The only thing that kept us in business was the savings your father had put aside and your dowry. Both are gone now."

Her dowry and the bookshop? That couldn't be right. It would mean Mrs. Shipton had lost Sarah's whole future in addition to the bookshop. "Are you saying that we have nothing?"

Mrs. Shipton nodded. "We have money enough to live on until the end of this month. After that..." She bowed her head against Sarah's arm and cried.

"Mother, what are you talking about?" Sarah asked the question as gently as she was able, but her mother wasn't making any sense. Sarah had personally kept the ledgers for the shop since her father died six months before, and had a hand in them for years prior. Everything had appeared to be in order.

"I'm so sorry," came the muffled reply. "I should have told you sooner. Now it's too late and we'll end up in the workhouse."

No, no, *no*. Sarah would do anything to keep that from happening...if it was even true. "The shop was making money when I left for Dover. What's happened since then?"

Sarah felt her mother take a deep breath and lift her face. "I made up a false ledger for you to work in when your father died and the shop began to lose money. And I hid some of the bills so you wouldn't worry about our finances."

False ledger? Hidden bills? "Then we really do have nothing."

And Sarah's whole future took on a shade of bleakness she'd only ever read about.

Mrs. Shipton nodded again, releasing her grip on Sarah to cover her face with both hands. Sarah rubbed her mother's back as her mind spun through possible solutions—she would deal with her mother's duplicity later. Her father was kin to a timber merchant in Birmingham, but there had been some sort of falling out and she was sure they'd find no help there. Her aunt in Dover was widowed and lived on a small annuity that only just met her needs, while Sarah's cousins worked to provide everything beyond the basics. They might be able to house Sarah's mother for a short time if Mrs. Shipton sold or let her house, but Sarah would have to find work quickly to keep from depleting her aunt's meager resources.

"Diana's ball." She hadn't meant to say the words aloud, but they popped into her head and out of her mouth with a tinge of despair. Diana Talbot had been Sarah's closest friend for the past nine years, and she was celebrating her recent betrothal with a ball given by her godfather, the Marquess of Preston. Sarah had been looking forward to the event for the past month, but how could she go now?

"Diana's ball," Mrs. Shipton repeated, lowering her hands into her lap. "It's tonight, isn't it?"

"It is."

"And your dress has already been paid for."

Where was her mother going with this? "It has."

"Then we have one hope left." Mrs. Shipton's eyes widened. "You can play Cendrillon and enchant a prince, a husband with wealth to save us."

That explained it—she'd been reading Perrault again. The story of Cendrillon and the handsome prince was one Mrs. Shipton had read to her daughter countless times in her own English translation when Sarah was younger, then in the original French as she grew older. It was naught but a fairy story, yet the happy marriage for the little cinder girl had captured Mrs. Shipton's heart.

"I doubt I'll enchant anyone in an evening, Mother."

"You are worried about your age and your dowry, but you forget that you are the great-granddaughter of an earl. You are every bit as well bred as Miss Talbot and her friends, and your education is far better than theirs."

At seven-and-twenty Sarah was no longer in the first blush of youth, and her lineage was less impressive among the *ton* than it was among her fellow shopkeepers. Combine those facts with her sudden lack of a dowry and she'd be lucky to find any husband at all, let alone a wealthy one. But her mother was right about her education, and her ability to run the bookshop should transfer well to running a home of any size. She would simply have to find a gentleman who valued such things.

Sarah gave herself a mental shake. How easy it was to become wrapped up in her mother's daydream. The far more practical plan would be to obtain a position as a clerk—if anyone would hire a female clerk—or a shop girl, or even a governess.

But aloud she said, "Yes, of course." The idea of Sarah meeting and marrying Society's equivalent of a handsome prince seemed to calm her mother, despite its improbability.

"Good." Mrs. Shipton sighed and wiped her eyes, her smile returning. "Then it's settled."

"Might I have a look at the ledger, Mother?" Sarah asked. "The real one, please. I'd like to see for myself what happened."

Her mother disappeared into the small back room and reemerged a few moments later with an account book the same size and color as the one Sarah had been poring over for the last several months. "Her you are, my dear. Though why you want to wade through all those numbers now is beyond me."

Though Mrs. Shipton had been a competent bookkeeper when her husband was alive, it was Sarah's father who had most often tended to the bookshop's finances. It was therefore possible that her mother was mistaken about how bad the situation was, and perhaps there was still a way to rescue the shop and keep their livelihood.

Sarah didn't say any of that aloud, though. She simply thanked her mother and collected the account books, taking them downstairs to study at the counter when there were no customers needing help.

But three hours later Sarah was no closer to saving the shop than she'd been when she arrived. The bell over the door *ting*ed and Diana entered, grinning and holding her arms out to her friend.

Sarah emerged from behind the counter to embrace her. "You're up early."

The contrast in their daily schedules was a running joke between them, and Diana chuckled. "I've been haunting the bookshop waiting for your return. I need your help making some last minute decisions for the ball."

"I'm so glad you're here," Sarah replied, giving her friend a tight squeeze before releasing her. "I could use your help as well."

"You first," Diana said, allowing Sarah to lead her to the counter. "Is it that steward you wrote me about?"

Sarah allowed herself a brief moment to picture him in her mind, walking her to her aunt's home. Then she pushed the thought away. "No, it isn't him. It's the shop." She glanced around to make sure the vicinity was empty of listening ears and lowered her voice. "I know it's vulgar to speak about money, but mother and I are about to lose our livelihood."

She told Diana about the shop's finances, gripping her friend's hand when she explained her mother's deceit with the false ledger. "I just can't believe she kept this from me—for six months! Even if I couldn't have helped the situation at all, I had a right to know what was going on. This affects my life just as much as it does hers."

"And now it's too late to save the bookshop."

It wasn't a question, but Sarah nodded anyway. "I think so. We can't afford to keep it open more than a few weeks, and that hurts almost as much as my mother's duplicity. My father opened this place just before I was born. I spent more of my childhood here than I did at our house."

"You poor dear. And here I was overwrought because the florist didn't have enough red roses for the ball."

Sarah managed a smile at that. "But red roses are your favorite."

"Yes, but I don't have to worry about living on the street." Diana reached out with her free hand and took Sarah's, squeezing them both. "You know I will help you any way I can."

But they both knew she could not offer enough money to alleviate the problem, having no coin to her name but the pin money her father allowed her. Her father or fiancé might help, but neither knew the Shiptons well enough to extend such an offer. It was not the done thing to speak of such matters with mere acquaintances.

"I do know, and I am grateful for it. I will certainly need your support in the coming days."

"That I will always give you."

"Good. I'm going to be in particular need of it after your ball. My mother has it in her head that I'll meet a wealthy gentleman who will marry me and solve all of our problems."

Diana giggled. "Wouldn't that be marvelous?"

Sarah sighed softly. "It would certainly take some of the weight from my mind. But I always wanted a marriage like my parents had—an affectionate partnership. I don't know if that could be achieved with a man I only just met, especially if he has to rescue me financially."

"It's not out of the realm of possibilities, though." The bell over the door sounded again as a customer entered, and Diana released Sarah's hands. "I shall return home and search through the guest list for some likely candidates."

"Diana..."

"If you find someone, your worries are over. And if you don't, well, there's no harm in trying."

Sarah bid her farewell and helped the new customer with a special order he'd placed, mulling over Diana's words. Perhaps it wouldn't be so bad to have a look at the gentlemen attending the ball. If her expectations were nonexistent to begin with, she couldn't be disappointed.

Andrew Elliott, Earl of Hartland ran a hand over his face as he entered Shipton's Books. He knew he looked presentable because his valet had refused to let him leave the house that morning without a bath and a change of clothes. Hart felt like something left behind on the boot scraper, though. The bright sunlight aggravated the pounding in his head, his empty stomach hovered somewhere between nausea and hunger, and he was having a difficult time keeping his eyes open. He'd either spent the past three days in a gaming hell or his workshop, and he honestly wasn't sure which it had been.

But Shipton's had specially ordered a collection of *The Emporium of Arts & Sciences* for him all the way from Philadelphia, and he'd been looking forward to its arrival for weeks. A good book—particularly a scientific one—would either settle his mind enough to allow him a good night's sleep or send him into another days-long spree in his workshop. If the former happened, perhaps the events of the last few days would come back to him. If it was the latter then he might end up with a new invention or blend of steel, and those could prove useful, too.

He also knew the proprietor's daughter would put aside an interesting volume or two for his perusal, and he was curious to see what she had for him today.

"Good afternoon, Lord Hartland."

"Good afternoon to you, Miss Shipton. Has my order arrived?"

"I believe I saw it in the back room when I came in this morning. Let me check."

He browsed the shelves for the few moments she was gone, then reciprocated the smile she wore upon her return. "It's here?"

"It is. And I had Mr. Higgins hold a copy of *Elements of Chemical Philosophy* for you when it came in, too. It was written by Sir Humphry Davy of the Royal Society."

Ah, she'd chosen well. Chemistry would put him right to sleep. "Davy? Isn't he the fellow who gave the paper on combining carbonic oxide and chlorine earlier this year?"

"It was his brother's paper, but yes, Sir Humphry is the one who presented it."

He picked up the book and leafed through a few pages. "Have you read it?"

"Yes."

"The paper or the book?"

Her smile widened a bare fraction of an inch. "Yes."

"What did you think?"

"I thought both brothers explained themselves in language that was easy to understand. One needs a bit of background in chemistry to appreciate the ideas being put forth, but one does not have to be an Oxford don for said ideas to make sense."

His eyes were back on the book in his hands. "Light reading, then."

"Compared to the rest of your library, yes."

Hart glanced up and caught a glint of amusement in her blue eyes. She would know about his library—she'd selected half of it for him. "Very well then, add it to my order."

He waited while she wrapped up the books for him then bid her good day, scanning the street outside the shop for his town coach. This was the last errand he needed to complete, and he was looking forward to draping himself across the coach seat for the short trip back to his estate in Hampstead.

There was no peace to be found at Elliot House, however. Hart's butler was waiting by the front door with a sealed letter on a salver.

"This came for you just after you left, my lord. It was the special messenger that delivered it."

"The special messenger" meant the letter was sent by someone in the unofficial intelligence gathering ring Hart belonged to, headed by the Earl of Wellington. The communications Hart received most often had something to do with a degenerate specimen of a man wreaking havoc in an area near one of Hart's estates. From time to time there was even the stink of treason on said specimen, and Hart was always relieved to see such men contained and dealt with appropriately. Even better when the population at large never knew they were in danger.

He handed over his hat and gloves, taking the letter from the butler and cracking the seal as he walked toward his study.

Hartland,

I haven't much time, so I'll keep this brief. A woman called Sarah Shipton has angered someone very powerful in Dover, and word has spread that this person is offering one hundred pounds to whomever kills Miss Shipton and provides proof of the deed. The proof is to be brought to a tavern called The Black Horse in Seven Dials as soon as may be, and payment will be offered anonymously. You know more people

Sarah Shipton? From the bookshop? How on earth had she managed to provoke a threat of death?

Hart scrubbed a hand through his short, dark hair and dropped onto the leather sofa in his study. He wasn't in the habit of letting information go to waste, nor of allowing ladies be killed. But what could he do here? His usual *modus operandi* was to put on one of the armor variations he'd crafted and go at the criminal head-on. But this time he didn't even know who the criminal was. And even if he did, it wouldn't matter; this criminal had authorized anyone and everyone to do his bidding. Taking just one person out of play wouldn't do any good.

The most straightforward action would be to return to the bookshop and tell Miss Shipton to leave Town. But how would he convince her to do so? He couldn't tell her about the intelligence gathering ring—only the eleven members and Wellington himself knew of its existence and they'd all been sworn to secrecy to protect each other. Perhaps he could tell her about the letter without revealing its origins? No, he doubted anyone would pick up and leave their home indefinitely based on the claims in a letter they couldn't verify.

He leaned his head back against the arm of the sofa, wishing he'd had more sleep. Or less wine. Whatever it was that was muddling his brain he now wished to perdition. Not that it would stop him the next time he went on a winning streak at cards or had a breakthrough with an invention, of course. But perhaps he wouldn't indulge again until Miss Shipton was out of harm's way.

What if he arranged for her to visit Paris? Or Milan? Or Dublin? He had friends in Dublin that could discretely see to her safety. Would she go if he presented it as her own version of the Grand Tour?

Hart must have drifted off to sleep, for the next thing he knew his valet was shaking him awake.

"I'm sorry, my lord, but you told me to make sure you looked your best tonight for Lord Preston's ball."

"What does that have to do with anything, Richards?" Hart asked, his eyes squeezed shut.

"You also told me you needed to leave by seven o'clock."

"And what time is it now?"

"A quarter past, my lord. I tried to wake you earlier, but you swung your fist at me and told me to go to the devil."

Hart turned onto his side and tried to bury his face in the leather of the sofa. "How quickly can you have my clothing ready?"

"It is ready now, my lord."

"Good man." He wasn't surprised. Richards had been with him for nearly two decades and was more than familiar with Hart's idiosyncrasies. "Just let me peel myself off the furniture and I'll be right up."

Forty-five minutes later Hart was greeting the Marquess of Preston and his goddaughter in the receiving line at Preston's home in fashionable Mayfair. He pasted on a smile for the sake of the lady and hoped he didn't look as bored as he knew he was about to feel.

Dancing turned out to be tolerable, particularly when he partnered one of his favorite merry widows and another just two sets later. Both seemed disappointed not to have secured a liaison with him, but Hart held firm. He enjoyed flirting with women, certainly, and pushing the bounds of propriety was enormously entertaining. But sometimes playing the libertine was more fun for him than actually being one, and it kept eligible ladies from thinking they might want to be the future Countess of Hartland.

"Lord Hartland?"

It was Preston's goddaughter...what was her name? Tiverton? Taggart? "Good evening, Miss Talbot. May I offer my congratulations on your engagement?"

"Thank you, my lord." She gave him a demure smile. "I'm glad that you were able to attend this evening. It means a great deal to my godfather."

"He wanted a crush for your celebration, no doubt, and the easiest way to get a large number of people in one place is to invite me." He waggled his eyebrows. "But I do wish you every happiness in your marriage."

Hart gave her a small bow and turned to go, but she caught his arm. "Might I have just one more moment of your time, my lord? There is someone I'd like to introduce to you."

He struggled to keep from rolling his eyes, but allowed her to turn him back around. If he fought the introduction he would lose more time than if he simply let it happen. "Certainly, Miss Talbot. It is your party, after all."

She kept a hold of his elbow and towed him a few steps toward a brunette in a pale green and silver gown. "Lord Hartland, this is my very good friend, Miss Shipton."

Well, here was an opportunity he couldn't pass up. Hart reached for Miss Shipton's gloved hand even though she hadn't offered it to him. "Yes, we've been acquainted with each other for many years, haven't we?"

"We have," she confirmed, taking back her hand. "Lord Hartland is a regular patron of my mother's bookshop."

"And a friend, too, I hope." Hart smiled at each lady in turn. "Are you engaged for the next set, Miss Shipton? Perhaps you would do me the honor?"

Miss Shipton's eyes darted from Hart's to Miss Talbot's then back again. "Certainly, my lord."

He took her gloved hand again and placed it on his sleeve, but instead of leading her toward the dance floor he headed for the ballroom door. Miss Shipton glanced back at her friend, but Hart leaned closer to her ear and said quietly, "I know this is unusual, but I must speak with you. Your life is in danger."

End of excerpt *The Good, The Bad, And The Scandalous* (The Heart of a Hero Series) by Cora Lee

Chapter One Excerpt from:

The Archer's Paradox
The Heart of a Hero Series

Chapter One

Romney Marsh, Kent
March 1812

COLIN HOSKINS MOVED to the window. There was nothing to see, but his instincts told him something wasn't right. It was bitterly cold and definitely too late for anyone to be about outside. Moving quickly, he went up the staircase to the watchtower he had built when he'd purchased the old manor house.

With its position along the coast, Romney Marsh was an ideal location for French agents to attempt to enter England. Though the other sheep farmers in the area thought him eccentric at best, he took his assignment from the Earl of Wellington seriously. That commitment included not letting on that he had been tasked to both gather intelligence and to ensure that no one entered the country through the marsh. The latest reports he had received indicated the French were focused on Russia, but that didn't preclude them from sending agents into England. In fact, an excellent time to do so would be when no one expected it.

His house was built atop a hill where it was less likely to flood, which also created an opportunity to see for miles in every direction. He reached the watchtower and a brief flash of light shone not far from shore. Seconds later, his guard dog gave a warning bark from below. Someone was on the beach. Reversing his path, he rushed back down the staircase and grabbed his quiver and bow, then exited out the front of the house, where Sampson greeted him. It had taken months for him to teach the Pyrenean Mountain Dog to not to bark excessively, but instead to give one signal bark when he sensed danger. Though his job was to keep the sheep safe, he also considered humans a threat to his flock, so he served to guard the house as well.

Together they moved down the hill toward the beach. Cold gusts of wind off the ocean coated them with sea spray. The bleat of a lamb sounded to his left and he stopped. Sampson stiffened, sniffing the air. He took his job of guarding the sheep quite seriously, especially during lambing season. It was a bit early yet for the lambs to be born, but it wasn't unheard of for them to begin birthing in early March, and a new born lamb would not survive a night outside in this weather. However, this wayward lamb did not belong to him. All of Colin's sheep were in the stable for the night.

Sampson took off down the hill to find the lamb and Colin followed behind at a slower pace, searching the coastline for signs of a lantern or the slightest flash of light where it shouldn't be. Though he didn't wish for the errant lamb to freeze on this cold night, he was more concerned about someone coming ashore. A sudden thought stopped him in his tracks. What if someone was using the lamb as a distraction to keep his attention away from nefarious activity elsewhere? Pulling an arrow out of his quiver, he nocked it to the bowstring and rushed down to the beach, splashing himself with cold water as he hit low patches in the marsh. A cloud shifted and the moon lit the shoreline. There was nothing there. No boat. Nothing out of the ordinary. Another scan of the visible parts of the beach revealed nothing. Either he had been mistaken about seeing the light earlier, or whoever landed on the beach had already escaped.

Another warning bark sent him racing back toward Sampson. Breathing heavily, he caught a flash of the white dog in the moonlight and slowed to a walk. Someone held a lantern up behind his dog, revealing the lamb in his mouth. As he drew closer, the outline of a woman's cloak took form.

"Is this your dog?"

What was a woman in formal dress doing traipsing around on the marsh? Her cloak was much too short for her and the shiny fabric of a ball gown shown below it.

"Yes."

"Will you please order it to drop my lamb?"

He stowed his bow and arrow and stopped a few feet from her.

"That would be counterproductive, I believe. Were you not attempting to catch the lamb?"

"Just like a man to underestimate the situation," she mumbled. "I don't wish to have the lamb injured."

"I should think not, but you have no reason to worry. Sampson is a very well trained guardian of livestock. He will not hurt your lamb, nor will he allow it to wander off again."

The clouds shifted and a patch of moonlight shone upon them. The bright green of her gown blended with the grass, aside from the mud caked on the hem. What was she doing out on the marsh, alone, at this time of night? In a ball gown, no less?

"Please allow me to introduce myself, Miss...?"

"I am Miss Pottinger, and this is my farm." She tilted her head to the house that lay about half a mile down the hill from their position.

Ah, that explained it. Mr. Pottinger had taken ill more than a year ago and was rarely seen outside even in summer, but surely there had to be someone in charge of this young lady who would soon notice her absence.

"Sampson." The dog immediately came to him and dropped the lamb at his feet. The creature was no worse for the wear except for a bit of slobber on his fleece. Colin picked it up and handed it to her.

"Thank you, Mr…"

"Hoskins." He cleared his throat and tried again. "I am Colin Hoskins. I live on the estate just above you."

"I see. Papa has not yet introduced me to all of the neighbors since I left school to join him. My apologies for not inviting you to the dinner party tonight, but it would've been very hard to send an invitation to a person of whose existence I was unaware."

He had to toss her words around in his head for a few moments before he could make any sense of them. A proper response likely didn't exist.

"Miss Pottinger, may I assist you in carrying your lamb back to the stable before it freezes?"

"There is no need. I am perfectly capable of carrying a tiny lamb." She muttered something else that he couldn't quite hear.

"I can only agree with your hypothesis. However, I offered to carry the lamb to save you from transferring anymore mud and slobber from the lamb to your gown."

"Oh." She glanced down at the streaks of muck across her abdomen. "Well, that was rather careless of me."

The strangeness of the situation swept over him. What if this odd girl was being used to distract him from whatever he had seen earlier? It was possible it had just been a fisherman, but he needed to search the beach as soon as possible and also learn more about this woman.

"Since you don't need any more assistance with the lamb, may I ask that you allow me to accompany you back to the house so I may wash the mud from my hands?"

"Of course. I need to bring this little hellion into the kitchen to warm him before giving him back to his mother." She cooed at the tiny creature. "Yes, I do. I'm sure your mother is very worried about you."

Colin thought otherwise. There were no frantic bleating noises coming from the stable, nor any other signs that the sheep were restless. There was definitely something suspicious going on. Having known Mr. Pottinger for years, Colin was certain he was not a threat, but that didn't mean his daughter couldn't have been persuaded or even tricked into helping French agents. He would have to watch their house until he could be sure.

She handed him the lamb and turned to head back down the hill.

"Miss Pottinger, may I ask where you lived prior to joining your father here?"

"I attended Madame Delacroix's School for Girls in London, then stayed on to teach French until Papa's condition deteriorated to the point that I needed to return home."

A teacher of French origin and a woman who was fluent in French. He needed more information about Miss Pottinger, that school, and its proprietor and other employees. Mr. Pottinger had been a tutor to the sons of several noble families prior to acquiring his farm, so it stood to reason that his daughter would be well educated, but Colin's instincts were telling him there was something more to this situation.

His boots squelched as they completed their wet, muddy journey down the hill. When they arrived at the Pottingers' home, the door stood ajar, which put him on edge immediately.

"Do you always leave your door open when you leave, Miss Pottinger?"

"Only when I'm chasing an escaped lamb and time is of the essence, Mr. Hoskins," she threw over her shoulder.

He gave Sampson the signal to stay, and the dog settled with his back against the house so he could keep watch. Colin removed his bow and quiver and followed her inside.

The moment they entered the house, she immediately went to the fireplace and threw a few pieces of wood onto the fire and placed the screen on the hearth. After a quick glance around the room, she removed the scarf from her head, took the lamb from him, and wrapped it tightly in the scarf before placing it on the hearth in front of the screen. Once the creature was settled, she washed her hands in a basin and gestured for him to do the same.

The first thing he noticed was her rather remarkable golden-red hair shining in the firelight. The second was her emerald green eyes. Her mother must have been stunning because though Mr. Pottinger was a good man, his daughter's beauty had not come from him. Coming to his senses and remembering his duties, Colin glanced around the large room that served as a kitchen, dining room, and parlor. There was no sign that a party, let alone any other gathering, had taken place that night. To his knowledge, Mr. Pottinger had only a woman who came from the village a few times a week to help him. Perhaps she had been hired to help with the party and had left while they were slogging about on the hill.

"Is your father about?" he asked.

"I fear he's already retired for the night, but I will give him your regards in the morning."

For a moment he thought she was going to ask him to leave, but then she surprised him by asking if he'd like tea. The house was quiet, peaceful even. Though he wasn't sensing any discomfort from her, that did not mean she was innocent. It was entirely possible she was a very good actress. He hung his rather wet cloak on a hook by the door.

She placed the tea service on the table and poured him a cup. "So, Mr. Hoskins, how did you come to live in Romney Marsh?"

"I planned to farm sheep, and this seemed like the best place to do so."

She nodded. "What did you do before you moved here?"

He narrowed his eyes. Her questions came across more like she was interrogating him than making polite conversation. "A great many things, but none of them compares to having a sheep farm."

Her eyes widened. "I shudder to think what you must've been doing before then, Mr. Hoskins."

He laughed—he couldn't help it. "What's wrong with sheep farming?"

"Nothing, it's just that it's hard work. Every time I turn around another lamb is escaping, and don't even get me started on harvesting the wool. Papa can sheer ten sheep in the time it takes me to finish one, and he never cuts them."

Hmm. Perhaps she really was just his daughter and not a threat if she was so familiar with sheep farming. "Is it just you and your father, Miss Pottinger, or do you have other siblings?"

She moved to the hearth to check on the lamb. "Two older sisters. Both married and living too far away to come visit us. At least that's what they say in their letters." She turned and met his eyes. "What about your family, Mr. Hoskins?"

"I don't have any family"

"None at all? No parents, siblings, wives, children?"

He nearly choked on a mouthful of tea. "No. And I'm not certain I want even one wife, let alone two."

She bit her lip in a rather appealing fashion, then smiled. "No, I don't suppose it would be much of an advantage to have two wives. They'd constantly be fighting to win your attention. One would be more than enough." With that, she commenced unwrapping the lamb.

"Miss Potter, have you had experience of a man with more than one wife?"

She shook her head. "Of course not, but I lived and worked at a school for girls. I also witnessed my father trying to keep both his mother and his wife happy, and it was definitely an uphill battle."

"I should think so." Normally he could judge a person's character almost immediately, but he was having trouble with Miss Pottinger. She was an enigma, and one he needed to solve. Her knowledge of human interaction made him wonder if she had received training somewhere. She was very astute for someone of her experience and background.

With the lamb in her arms, she moved to leave the house.

He retrieved his wet cloak and opened the door for her. "This is my cue to leave. I thank you for the tea, Miss Pottinger."

"You're quite welcome, Mr. Hoskins. Thank you for your help with the lamb."

He whistled to Sampson and headed up the hill far enough that his dog went back to his station outside his stable. Once he was certain she couldn't see him in the darkness, he circled back toward the house and sought the window to her father's bedchamber. It was possible that she wasn't his daughter at all. She might be a French operative who killed him and was masquerading as his daughter. This house would be the perfect place to plan and execute an invasion.

The first window he peered through was an empty bedchamber, and the second was a parlor. Thankfully the house wasn't overly large and consisted of one story only. Snores sounded from the next chamber he came upon. A quick glance revealed the rather broad outline of Mr. Pottinger. Colin breathed a sigh of relief. There was still a chance that she really was Pottinger's daughter and that she might be trustworthy.

He continued his circuit round the house so he could return home along a path that wasn't visible to others. There was one more window. He ought not to look, but he couldn't help himself. The fire burned brightly in the chamber, illuminating everything. Miss Pottinger reached over her shoulder to unfasten her gown, and he itched to offer his assistance. It was an arduous task for her, but would take him no time at all. Once she freed a few of the buttons, the gown slid down her slim figure. Her corset went next, though it was unlike any he had ever seen, and he had seen his fair share. Usually a lady could not remove her own corset without assistance, but she had modified it so the laces were along her side and allowed her to remove it on her own. Unfortunately, the shadows cast by the flickering fire obscured his view. That was, until she turned, showing off her full silhouette. The firelight highlighted all of her curves and hollows while she stood in nothing but her shift. He swallowed and sucked in a deep breath, trying to control his reactions. Good grief. He was the worst sort of Peeping Tom. He turned and stalked away before he lost the willpower to leave without finding out if she slept in the nude.

By the time he made his way up the hill, Sampson had settled into his place in front of the closed doors of his stable. Try as he might, Colin could not get the animal to stay in the stable with the livestock. Every time he tried, the dog barked incessantly until Colin freed him. Granted, with his double layered coat he never seemed to be cold outside regardless of the weather, but it still didn't sit well with Colin to leave an animal exposed to the elements. For now, he was glad the dog would be on watch until he figured out whether Miss Pottinger was a threat. To that end, he entered the house and went straight to his study where he poured himself a very large amount of brandy and sat down to write a request to Captain Grant Alexander for as much information as he could find about Miss Pottinger and Madame Delacroix's School for Girls.

End of excerpt *The Archer's Paradox* (The Heart of a Hero Series) by Ally Broadfield

Prologue and Chapter One Excerpt from:

The Missing Duke
The Heart of a Hero Series

Copyright © 2017 Heather King

Prologue

London 1788

"MARY, I HAVE a message for you from Nurse Wilson." Mrs. Ashperton came bustling into the nursery, the words already falling from her lips. "She is sadly indisposed and you are to take the twins to the park in her stead. Francis will accompany you."

"Very good, Mrs. A," Mary replied. Lowering her eyes to hide a grin, she bobbed a slight curtsey. What a stroke of luck.

"I will have less of your impertinence, girl, if you please. That is Mrs. Ashperton to you and don't you forget it." Although her words were severe, the housekeeper's tone was mild. "The carriage has been ordered. Mind you dress the boys warmly; there is a cool breeze this morning."

"Yes... Mrs. Ashperton." Her thoughts on the handsome new footman, Mary gazed across the bright, spacious room to where the young Marquis and his brother were playing quietly before the fire. Would she have time to redo her hair?

"Well, don't stand there wool-gathering!" the housekeeper exclaimed tartly, the ribbons on her cap bobbing as if to add their insistence. "Get their faces and hands washed and tidy them up. The sons of a duke cannot go out with their breakfast stuck to their cheeks!"

Within the hour, Mary had duly made the two small boys presentable, wiping away egg yolk, brushing hair and dressing them in skeleton suits of nankeen trousers, warm stockings and matching blue jackets with natty little caps. Although twins, they were not identical, the young Marquis having dark hair while his brother had the colouring of a bronze statue. In fact, they bore little resemblance to each other at all, leading to unfounded whispers below stairs that her Grace had accommodated two sires. Mary found the time to put her own hair into a knot before donning her best hat and cloak. It was important she make the most of this opportunity and reflect well on the Duke's household, she told herself. It had nothing to do with Francis whatsoever.

They mounted into the low, gilt-embossed children's carriage, drawn by a matched pair of golden dun ponies and brought around to the front of the house by one of the grooms. Francis jumped on to the rear step and the equipage set off smoothly in the direction of Hyde Park. The short drive from Berkeley Square took only a few minutes, and soon the carriage had entered the park by the Chesterfield Gate and was bowling along beneath an avenue of walnut trees. Mary directed the groom to halt beside a stretch of level meadow on the approach to the Cheesecake House.

"Thank you," she said, smiling warmly at Francis when he lifted her two charges down. He grinned back and her heart jumped.

The groom gave a disinterested sniff and she quickly turned away. As he clicked at the ponies to move off again, a large town chariot overtook and a lone rider ambled past. The horseman gave them a cursory, sideways glance as his sorry nag continued along the driveway without seeming to require any direction. Beyond noting his working attire and taking him for an ostler or jockey from Tattersall's, Mary paid him no further mind. A low wooden rail separated the park from the carriageway and, having negotiated this obstacle, she led the boys across the grass to a tall elm perched on a slight rise. Francis spread a blanket on the ground and while their lordships ran about firing pretend arrows and riding imagined, spirited chargers, Mary sat down, carefully arranging her grey skirts about her. The footman leaned one shoulder against the tree and chuckled.

"This certainly beats cleaning clothes and polishing the silver," he remarked.

"Yes, until those rascals get into mischief," she answered. "Last week, Nurse Wilson gave me a bear-garden jaw because Master Adam was running about the nursery with her sewing shears. I had turned my back for less than a minute, I swear."

"Mr. Ashperton made me clean all the silver again on Sunday, just because I missed one tiny speck of paste. All of it. Have you any idea how much silver tableware there is in his pantry? I only got about two hours' sleep that night."

"I rarely get much more than that," she said, peering sideways at him in a coquettish fashion. "I share with Maud, the under-housemaid, and she snores!"

He laughed. "I wonder if Mrs. Ashperton does, too. That might explain Mr. A's perpetual frown."

"Ooh, you wicked thing!" Mary brought her hand to her mouth, pretending to be greatly shocked. She could tell by the twinkle in his eyes he was not deceived.

He pushed away from the gnarled trunk. "Would you care for a cheesecake?"

"Are you offering to buy me one?" She made her tone deliberately coy.

In response he held out his arm, crooked at the elbow. "I had a bit of luck on the horses. I can stretch to a tart or two."

"Lead on, then, fine sir," she trilled, dipping a mock curtsey. "Master Robert, Master Adam, come along now, please!"

They walked the short distance to the timber-framed cottage. Set in its own grounds behind a stout wooden fence, it nestled among mature shrubs and trees. Holding the two boys by the hand, Mary followed Francis across a sturdy timber footbridge to the front door of the house. The landlord was standing on the threshold, wiping his hands on his apron. He greeted them cheerfully.

"Good morning. It is a fine one, is it not?"

"It is indeed," replied her companion. "Two half measures of cider and four of your finest cheesecakes, landlord, if you please. Only the best is good enough for the sons of dukes out on a spree."

"Oho, like that, is it?" The man rubbed his round stomach and chuckled. "They seem determined young sprigs, so they do. You look to have your work cut out there, missy. Would you be their nursemaid, then?"

Mary glared at Francis. "I believe that is for me to know, good sir. I am not sure my employer would wish for the world to be privy to his sons' excursions in the pursuit of exercise," she said, copying Nurse Wilson's manner in as haughty a tone as she could manage.

The landlord, looking taken aback, stared at her for a moment. Then, with a wink at Francis, he tipped her an ironic bow and said:

"My apologies, my lady, I was not aware I was addressing royalty. Would you care to step into my parlour?" He waved his arm in the direction of a pair of small, round tables which had been set on a square of dandelion-riddled grass. Several chickens clucked and scratched nearby, two under one of the tables. They squawked indignantly and flapped away at the small party's approach. The young Marquis ran after one with a white body and black tail feathers. He tried to pick it up, but it opened its beak, squawked again and with its wings beating wildly, leaped out of his reach.

"Master Robert, come and sit down, please." Mary called him to order. "Master Adam, if you pick up that worm, you will have no cheesecake!"

The landlord reappeared bearing a large tray, and set before them their refreshments. The cheesecakes at this house were renowned and looked delicious, being speckled brown with nutmeg atop a creamy filling and encased in golden pastry. Mary took a small bite. The rich, almond custard almost melted on her tongue and the pastry was crisp and light.

"Oh," she murmured, "that is glorious."

Francis grinned and wolfed a third of his in one enormous mouthful. Chewing as he spoke, he asked:

"You never had one before?"

"Not from here," she clarified, trying not to laugh at the comical contortions of his face as he endeavoured to collect a crumb of pastry from the corner of his mouth. "'Tis a special treat to eat in the park."

"I do not like it," declared Master Robert. "It is nasty. I want to go to the lake. I want to see the ducks!"

"You may see the ducks shortly," she told him. "Sit still and wait quietly, please. A young gentleman must learn not to make a fuss in public. Master Adam, I will not tell you again. Throw that worm away and come here so I may wipe your hands. You can't eat with soil all over them."

"Yes, I can!" he retorted. "My papa is a duke. I can do whatever I want and you cannot stop me!"

He threw the worm away, as she had demanded, but not under the bush where he had found it. He launched it straight at her.

Mary squealed in surprise and jumped up, brushing at herself with her hands.

"You little beast!" she cried. "Come here!"

With Francis doubled up with laughter, she ran after Adam, who galloped away across the small garden, shrieking in delight.

"You cannot catch me! You cannot catch me!" he sang.

"Is that so?" Mary caught up her skirts and chased after the dodging and weaving child.

Francis almost fell off his chair and slapped his hand on the table as he righted himself.

"Come on, Mary! Is that the best you can do? He's running rings around you!"

The chickens scattered, speckled beads of white, brown and black on green velvet. Not to be outdone, Robert scurried after them. Giggling merrily, Adam scampered off in the opposite direction, towards the wood beyond the house. By now caught up in the game and laughing almost as much as the rest of them, Mary followed him.

"You wait until I get a-hold of you, Master Adam. You'll be sorry!"

The little boy gave a startlingly good imitation of a neighing horse, leaped in the air like a battle charger and cavorted in between the trees. Mary could hear his footsteps crunching on dead leaves and bits of wood. Then everything went silent.

"Adam?" she called, suddenly concerned. If anything happened to him she could lose her position. He was in her care. "Adam, are you all right?"

She ran to the place where she had last seen him and peered into the shadows. There was no sign of him. Heart thumping, she pushed through a clump of undergrowth. Her bonnet snagged on a hawthorn branch and was pulled askew.

"Adam! Answer me! Where are you?"

Without warning, he poked his head around the trunk of a tall chestnut tree a few yards from her and stuck out his tongue.

"Here I am!"

"Oh, you did give me a fright! Come along now, please."

"Not till you catch me!"

"I'll catch you a clip round the ear is what I'll do, young man, if you don't do as you are told."

"I shall tell Papa and you will be put in gaol," he retorted. He skipped out of sight again and she heard his light, boyish gurgles of laughter dancing about the wood as fireflies might dance on a summer's eve. It was a long-ago memory, yet cherished still; sitting about her grandfather's campfire the night before his last drove to Wales. He had not returned, a week of torrential rain having ended his days through a grievous inflammation of the lungs, and Mary's mother had brought her to London. Forced on to the streets to survive, her mama had died from the pox. There was little she would not do to avoid that fate, she thought now, and humouring a small child, however spoilt, took no great effort.

Pinning a wide smile to her lips, therefore, she chanted, "Eight, seven, six, five, four... three, two, one. I'm coming, whether you are ready or not!"

Several minutes later, her sombre mood had left her and she began to laugh with genuine amusement again, the impromptu game of hide-and-seek coming to a satisfactory conclusion when she found Adam caught in a knot of brambles. They walked back towards the picnic lawn where they had left Francis and Robert.

A pewter tankard stood upon the second table, the only evidence of another's presence. A quick glance as she and Adam passed told Mary that the vessel was empty, just the dregs remaining. Francis was sprawling back in his chair, his ankles resting on the edge of their own table, which was littered with crumbs and empty plates. He had eaten the remaining cheesecakes and was gently snoring. Of Lord Robert there was no sign.

"Francis!" Mary ran to his side and shook him. "Wake up! Where is Master Robert?"

He blinked a few times and rubbed his face. "He was here a moment ago."

"A moment ago, you say? How long have you been sleeping?"

"I wasn't asleep."

"Oh!" She pushed at his ankles. As they dropped to the ground, he lost balance and the chair toppled over with a crash, taking him with it. "There was somebody else here. Look," she said, pointing at the tankard. "Did you see him? What did he look like? Did you see which way he went?"

Francis climbed laboriously to his feet and sniffed. "I didn't see nuthin'," he answered in a belligerent tone. "What about you? You are the one supposed to be lookin' after the little—"

"Watch your tongue!" she interrupted. "Little pitchers have ears too!"

"Ha? What pictures? What are you wittering about, now? We're outside. There ain't no pictures out here." He seemed nervous, as well he might. His speech was no longer quite so smooth as it had been.

"Oh, get out of my way! We have to find him. Anything could have happened."

"He'll just have wandered off, that's all."

She turned and glowered at him. "You go into the house and discover if anyone has seen him, then check the nearby paths. He could have wandered anywhere." She paused, thinking. "He wanted to see the ducks. Find the carriage and ask Evans to help us search. I will take Master Adam and look down by the lake."

"Yes, my lady!" Francis jumped to attention and gave a parody of a salute.

"Aw, stop acting the dimber-cove, you ain't no knight of the rainbow! Go parley with the reader merchants and find out if they know anything," she retorted, lapsing into the cant that had been so much a part of her youth.

For a moment Francis gaped at her; then, without a word, he spun on his heel and ran into the Cheesecake House. Taking Adam's hand, Mary almost dragged him past the heavy wooden entrance door, around the end of the house and through a shrubbery of mixed trees and large bushes to the lakeside. A pair of ducks was floating on the calm green surface a few feet from the sandy shore. One bobbed its head beneath the water and came back up with some aquatic weed in its beak. The other flapped its wings before settling again. Neither seemed particularly disturbed.

Mary scanned the ground. At first she saw nothing to give her pause, merely a host of boot prints and the occasional cigar stub. She led Adam along the bank behind the cottage, passing a small wooden jetty. Two men were sitting in a rowing boat more than two-thirds of the way across the water, one wielding the oars with a somewhat jerky motion, it seemed, for the boat tipped and rocked as it went. They were already out of earshot and since there was no sign of Robert or any other figure in the craft, she turned her attention back to the riverside ahead of her.

Adam tugged at her hand. "Want to go home, now," he said, his bottom lip curling into a pout.

She bent down to him. "We cannot go home until we find Robert. He is hiding somewhere and we have to look for him. Where would you hide, if you were him?"

Shading her eyes from the bright spring sunshine, she stared up ahead. Beyond the fence surrounding the house, and dissected by one of the carriage drives, rough parkland stretched to the parade ground. Farther away, woods lined the valley of the Tyburn brook. There was no-one to be seen, let alone a small boy.

Then Adam, who had been contorting his face in careful thought, appeared to make up his mind, for he began to pull her in the other direction. As they drew level with the ducks and with the sunshine behind her, Mary spotted a smaller footprint she had previously missed, at the edge of the sand shore where it blended into the grassy footpath. The path also crossed over the moat spanned by the footbridge and followed the bank of the lake.

"Shall we run, Adam?" she intoned in a sing-song voice to hide her rising concern. "Let's find where Robert is hiding."

They ran perhaps a hundred yards. Mary's gaze swept back and forth as they went. There was a pool a little further on, bordered by reeds and clumps of rough grass. Beyond the pond, the bank curved around the end of the lake, where earth had been piled to dam the original brook when the Serpentine had been created. Now it was home to a forest of dark and brooding trees. She swallowed and slowed her pace. The spot was well known for deaths. The waters here were filthy and deep. Sewage released into the river collected around the sluice. An iron railing extended along the footpath above the sluice, but was not enough to prevent either the various suicides or bathing accidents which had occurred in recent times. Built by the architect, a waterfall took the river's overflow into another pond beyond the dam. There were dangers everywhere for an adventurous small boy.

Suddenly, Adam stopped, jerking his hand from Mary's.

"Look!" he cried, pointing.

She returned her glance to the footpath in front of them, following the line of his arm. Caught in a thicket, at the edge of the steep bank above the water, was Robert's jaunty blue cap.

Chapter One

London 1814

"AND THEN, LUCIEN, my good fellow," continued Lord Adam Bateman, tapping a sheaf of papers on the library table in front of him, "I wish you to take a hackney into the City and deliver this letter to my man of business. Mr. Liversedge has requested some personal information with respect to my brother and I do not care to entrust it to a messenger, nor yet even one of the footmen."

"Very good, sir. So, if I might be so bold as to enquire, your brother was never found?" His voice was light. It matched his slight build but bordered on the effeminate.

"No, he was not." Adam considered his secretary, debating how much to tell him. He was young, fair and very enthusiastic. Fresh down from Oxford and newly appointed to the post on the recommendation of Mr. Liversedge, the youth was proving diligent and efficient. He had given his age as one-and-twenty, but appeared much younger. "An extensive search was carried out. My father had every blade of grass overturned, it seems, as well as men on the lake, dredging to the bottom with long poles. No trace was found beyond his cap," he revealed at last. "My nursemaid said she saw a rowing boat on the far side of the lake, but again, neither it nor the two men supposedly in it were discovered."

"Yet you still believe the Duke is alive?"

"Yes, I do; with every fibre of my being. No doubt that sounds the stuff of madness to you, but I assure you there is no necessity to have me committed to Bedlam! My brother and I are twins. Twins have a special bond, one which others cannot ever know. Were he dead, I should know it, deep within." Feeling somewhat foolish, he tapped his chest. "This is why, now my father has died, I will not take the title. Indeed, I cannot. There is no reason to suppose he is dead. I will be as the Prince Regent is for the King; I will be the acting Duke of Wardley, in that I will oversee my brother's estates and concerns on his behalf until such time as I am assured he is truly no longer alive."

He stood up and walked across to the window. A long garden led to the ducal mews, hidden behind a high brick wall. The wall was bathed in warm spring sunshine and barely visible for a riot of reddish purple honeysuckle stems just beginning to come into flower. Beneath it was a wrought-iron seat and a stone sun-dial. He swallowed a lump which rose in the back of his throat. Young as they had been, Robert had been fascinated by the instrument and the movement of the sun, an interest their father had fostered.

Robert could not be dead. It was simply not conceivable. It was why Adam had dedicated his whole life to the search for him and why he had made the long journey to Ireland six years ago, at the behest of Sir Arthur Wellesley, as his Grace had been then. It was why he had joined Wellington's secret intelligence brigade at that gathering of like-minded men in the home of the Earl of Hartland. Yet what could have been the motive for kidnap? No ransom note had ever been received – or if it had, his father had taken the knowledge with him to the grave.

Sighing, Adam turned back to face the room. It was a calm, restful place. He withdrew here whenever the pressures of being the Duke of Wardley's younger brother became more than he could bear. The walls were yellowing to cream with age and smoke; the furniture was solid walnut and leather. Bookcases lined two walls, filled with reassuring, leather-bound tomes covering fascinating topics of the arts, the classics, sciences, law, religion and many more – more than a man could read in several lifetimes. He could lose himself in here for days, he mused, if only duty – and his mother – would allow him to do so.

The secretary had twisted around in his chair and was regarding Adam gravely without uttering a word. Once more in command of himself, Adam cleared his throat.

"I made myself a promise I would keep searching until I found him, one way or the other. It leads me into some nefarious places... and on occasion I overhear conversations... snippets of information which might benefit others. I will ask you to forget what I have just told you – I do so only so you might be prepared should sensitive questions ever be asked."

"I understand completely, sir." The secretary paused for a moment. "In the notes I was copying yesterday, I read there were three servants charged with the care of you and the Duke on that fateful morning; your nursemaid, a footman and a groom."

"That is correct."

"May I enquire what happened to them? I assume they were dismissed?"

"Not Evans – the groom. He is now the under-coachman. He was in charge of the carriage and was not responsible for our care. The other two were discharged from service, but my father was lenient and did not prosecute them for negligence, according to my mother."

"Have – forgive me if I speak out of turn – have they been located? There might be some information they remembered afterwards or did not divulge at the time which might help."

"No, I do believe I had not considered that. We must rectify the omission."

"Do you remember the boat the nursemaid saw? I realize you were very young, but sometimes children retain such details, I am told."

"You seem uncommonly interested in this matter."

The youth fingered the narrow band of lace at his cuff. "I beg your pardon, my lord, if I appear overly inquisitive. My intention was only to be of assistance."

"There is no need to apologize. You are very young to be concerned with something which happened so long ago, that is all." He stopped, deliberating. "I have a vague recollection of an old rowing boat pitching on the water, but I cannot tell you if it is a genuine memory or more a matter of the maid's assertions having been repeated."

The secretary picked up a notebook from the desk before him and sifted through its pages.

"At the time, Evans stated he saw 'a ruffianly fellow watching the two boys with undue interest as he rode past when they were playing in the meadow.' Could this person perhaps have been in league with either the nursemaid or the footman, or indeed, both?"

Adam considered this. After a moment he shook his head. "No, it is unlikely. It was the first time Mary, the nursemaid, had been in charge of us in the park. She had no prior knowledge of the excursion. Nurse Wilson had been taken ill that morning."

"The footman, Francis Mead, had but recently been taken on, I understand?"

"I believe so. Mr. and Mrs. Ashperton were responsible for the hiring of household servants. They were noted for the high standards they demanded from the other servants, whilst being scrupulously fair. I cannot imagine they would have taken on anyone without good references."

"Nevertheless, sir, it is an avenue which should perhaps be investigated. Given sufficient reason, people will do or say things they might otherwise not." His voice rose towards the end of the sentence. He coughed and continued in a gruffer tone, "As I can attest from my experiences while up at Oxford, young men are prone to... distraction from certain... low pursuits. If, perchance, he owed someone money..." He allowed his voice to fade away and straightened a quill in the standish in front of him.

Adam looked at him curiously. Was the lad blushing? Well, well! Perhaps there was more to his quiet secretary than he had first supposed.

"Indeed, I can attest to that myself!" he remarked with a laugh. "Fortunately, I had a generous allowance – and a father usually well disposed towards bailing me out of difficulties, even if it cost me a thunderous jobation. You make an excellent point, my boy. I confess to having concentrated my energies on seeking information on the boat, the men in it and the fellow riding by."

The secretary lifted his gaze from his desk. Large blue eyes, suspiciously luminous, surveyed him. Downy, golden lashes framed them, fanning over the youth's pale cheek. They were far too pretty for a man, he reflected. He must beware not to send the boy to any rough places in his stead or Robert might not be the only one to disappear without a trace into London's underworld. Giving his head a quick shake to dispel such thoughts, he forced his mind back to the present.

"I can make some enquiries for you, my lord."

"Yes." Adam returned to the library table. "I think we must widen the field of enquiry. As you suggest, there may be some connection to the servants. It is possible they were innocent of any wrong-doing, yet were somehow duped."

"I further read in your notebooks of the late Duke's belief that his adversary in the quest to progress the science of ballooning was somehow responsible for his heir's disappearance. You do not appear to have supported that theory."

Adam sighed. "No. I cannot think it to be true. The Earl of Brandford and my father had a bitter rivalry at times, but such an action is not to be thought of. So far as I am aware, Brandford is an honest man. He fought beside Grosvenor at the Siege of Copenhagen, and early on in the Peninsular campaign. His son and I were at Eton together. If I remember rightly, the Earl's fascination with balloons was from a military aspect. He believed they could be used to oversee enemy movements on the battlefield. There is such an obsession, though – a mania, almost – amongst those desirous of taking to the skies, I daresay there were others with fewer scruples."

"With your permission, sir, my father's shop lies not far from Mr. Liversedge's office. It is remarkable what a tailor hears during the course of pursuing his trade. My brother also employs two apprentices and a boy to make deliveries. The markets are full of gossip. If I might call upon my family while I am in the City, I may be able to seek another path or two."

"Do so, Lucien, with my goodwill. Anything you may discover can only be better than having a blank page to consider."

End of excerpt *The Missing Duke* (The Heart of a Hero Series) by Heather King

Chapter One Excerpt from:

The Mercenary Pirate
The Heart of a Hero Series

Chapter One

Saint-Malo, France, September 1812

NOTHING DREW MORE suspicion than a lone wolf scouting for his pack.

Wolfgang entered *La Guêpe*—the Wasp—and took in the scene unfolding in the tavern, reaping uninvited attention from those who glanced his way.

"It's the captain of the *Sea Wolf*!" someone shouted.

Chairs screeched against the floorboards in the smoky din. Voices stopped mid-conversation. Several men ignored the disruption his entrance was causing, continuing to brawl in the corner. One bumped into a corsair, who became so enraged that he grabbed the unfortunate man by his neck and snapped it. The gamblers who were spread throughout the Wasp ignored the murder without flinching. They merely continued to cast bets on the mounting caches in the center of rough-hewn tables. It was a testament to the level of violence typically found in places like these. And Wolf thrived on it.

Saint-Malo was a stronghold with a centuries-old reputation as a den of disreputable pirates. Wolf had docked there on several occasions while participating in free trade and rendezvousing with contacts from the two secret intelligence-gathering organizations he worked for—Wellington's spies and the Legion, a group operating under Lord Fynes that hunted down those responsible for undermining British rule and funding

Napoleon's war, in particular a man or group known simply as *Typhon*.

Wolf's habits and tracking skills—a talent he'd perfected while living with Indians in the Colonies—had been useful in scouting Marshal Marmont's activities in the Battle of Salamanca. Since then, Marmont had withdrawn to Madrid, giving Wolf leeway to travel to the coast and sail to Saint-Malo where another one of Wellington's agents was waiting to pass along information he'd been promised about his long-lost brother's whereabouts. The investigatory work done on Wolf's behalf was supposed to lead him to his brother, Kearney, who he hadn't seen since he'd received a head injury at age eight on the docks in Bristol, an injury that had erased his earlier childhood memories.

The air crackled with tension inside the tavern, drawing Wolf's attention back to the present and reeking of tobacco, stale malty ale, body odor, and a hint of desperation. Wolf didn't favor this particular tavern as the men who frequented it were Malouines. Few of these men who hailed from Saint-Malo did not take to sea, and they certainly never counted the odds against themselves. They'd been bred to raid Spanish and British ships, and they shirked every decency known to man. He was accustomed to the stares and the fear he provoked; it was treatment shown him no matter the port or establishment. Disregarding potential threats—like him—tended to get people killed.

Smoke plumed from his cigar as he chewed on the fermented end of the dark tobacco wrapper, trying to hide his contempt. Wolf didn't abide complications. Seedier establishments offered more privacy than the lofty clubs fellow members of Wellington's ring—Lords Hartland, Thorston, Bateman, and St. Peter—frequented. Being willing to go where the titled dared not go made Wolf invaluable, and appreciated men did not vanish without a trace. Competence and cunning kept men alive.

Wolf waited none too patiently for the crowd to sate its collective curiosity. When his audience finally lost interest in him and focus returned to the evening's entertainment of gambling and sensual pursuits, Wolf took the spicy, peppery Portuguese cigar from between his lips with his thumb and forefinger as he searched the crowd for the man he'd come to meet.

He bared his teeth. He'd been in Wellington's employ for four years, and during all that time, the world had been at war and Typhon had been at large. One mission had led to another and another without Wolf ever receiving what he'd been promised at the onset of his joining the Legion. *Bollocks*. He'd served his purpose. He'd fought with honor, killing only when necessary, though the demon inside him yearned to cut his enemies to ribbons, while information about his brother dangled temptingly out of reach.

Anger reared its ugly head, not for the first time—or the last, he wagered.

"*Je ne veux pas de problème!*" a small, defiant voice shouted. *I don't want any trouble.*

Who did? Wolf grumbled to himself, beset by the lack of empathy that enveloped his senses. The stranger shouting to his left mirrored his own thoughts. Trouble always managed to find Wolf.

With Wellington's army entrenched around the Castile at Burgos and Wolf's men waiting for orders aboard his ship, the *Sea Wolf*, he didn't have time for distractions. He proceeded forward with a slow, purposeful, and steady gait, ignoring the scuffling to his left as he made his way through the crowded interior to the bar where a winking barmaid displaying her ample breasts to full advantage.

The tempting French woman was not who she claimed to be, however. The name Jolie was one of Joanna Pearson Devlin's better-known aliases. She was the wife of Michael Devlin, the Demon of Dublin's Hell, and an ally. Joanna and the Earl of Hartland had been pivotal in organizing Wellington's British intelligence ring. It was she who had recruited him four years ago after spotting him earning stake money in a boxing match in Bristol. His roughened edges, streetwise fighting abilities, and roving lifestyle had been an asset when Wellington campaigned outside England and critical information needed to be passed from one country to another.

"Why, if it isn't the *Sea Wolf*." She batted her eyelashes, continuing her ruse and taking no chances that someone might overhear their conversation.

"Jolie." He regarded her over the smoke coiling from his cigar and nodded in acknowledgment.

Joanna was a minx who had a way of switching characters like adorning a new gown. It was a necessary talent when it came to survival in their business.

But Joanna and their fellow spies weren't Wellington's first operatives of espionage. Wolf had come from the Battle of Salamanca mere weeks after Wellington's cunning Scotsman Colquhoun Grant had been captured and taken to Bayonne. He'd left the keen-eyed Scot Andrew Leith-Hay and nobleman

Charles Cocks to accompany Wellington and his army to the Castile at Burgos.

Wolf bowed his head slightly. "To what do I owe this pleasure?"

"A reunion of sorts, *Monsieur*," she purred. "It has been a long time, no? But first, you look weary. What can I serve you?"

Joanna knew very well that Wolf wanted information on his brother, Kearney. Hadn't that been what Wellington had promised him? His services had been successfully acquired because of that promise. Though Wolf enjoyed serving his country without complaint, he had already waited four years to find out where his brother was. And after what Wolf had endured in Salamanca, he expected payment for services rendered.

"Give me a beer," he said.

Joanna turned around and reached for the large barrel positioned behind her as Wolf leaned his elbows on the counter. To serve Wellington, he'd turned his back on Captain Franco Charve in a tavern similar to this one. The cut had cost him plenty, including Franco himself, the man who'd plucked him out of the mud, the father figure Wolf had been denied during his murky childhood. The little he could recall—images of his elusive brother and the haunting guilt that plagued him—filled him with dread.

In the meantime, he had nothing to show for his involvement with Wellington or the Legion.

The scuffling and grunts grew louder, making Wolf curious. He peered over his shoulder at the crowd that was encircling someone in their midst, his leather overcoat straining as he moved.

"You heard me. Stay . . . back!" the voice shouted again.

Wolf's sluggish heartbeat began to race as concern washed over him. He straightened, a tingling weight building in his chest.

He narrowed his eyes and cut them to the corner where the voice had originated from. His instincts called him out, and his nerve endings blazed to life as he tensed for a fight. This time, there was no mistaking the fear he heard in the voice or the slight feminine tone that was prickling his senses. A boy, perhaps? Or...

Bollocks! Surely those men weren't beating a woman on the premises?

"*Monsieur*?" Joanna asked when he didn't acknowledge the beer she placed before him. "What is happening over there is none of your concern. We have more important matters to discuss. Hart—"

"Can take care of himself," Wolf said. The man was an earl, and his homes, medieval Hartland Abbey in Devon, Glanmire House in Cork, and Elliot House in Hampstead, were veritable strongholds. Hartland had titled peers, plus Captain Alexander, Major Bannerman, Michael Devlin, and Colin Hoskins to help the Legion uncover Typhon's true identity. "Whatever he needs from me can wait."

Restless now and completely ill at ease, Wolf turned around and headed toward the crowd of men while everyone else attempted to mind their own business. Thirst came second to the protective urges clamoring inside him. His instincts had never failed him before. And right now, he was sure the voice he'd heard wasn't from a mere boy but a young woman who was but moments away from losing her life.

Wolf placed his cigar between his lips once more. He marched back the way he'd come, shoving his way through the derelict group, men clothed in shabby threads that appeared to have never seen water or soap. In their midst, he finally clearly observed the owner of the raspy voice. It seemed to be a small, disheveled boy, after all. The lad boasted a bloody lip and a swollen eye. He was chained to a wall, bracing himself against his attackers, knees bent, fists out in front of him, prepared to take on the horde.

A filthy mop of hair half covered the boy's face as he glared through the strands. Wolf narrowed his eyes on the captive, studying him carefully. Regardless of whether the child was incredibly brave or terribly unwise, Wolf was almost certain this boy was not who he appeared to be. A lot of care seemed to have been taken to alter the stranger's physical shape, but the filth couldn't completely hide the facial bone structure that made him revert to his earlier belief that he was looking at a young woman, who for some reason was masquerading as a boy. But who was she? And how had she gotten here?

Chains rattled as she moved, the sound horrifyingly familiar as flashes of his childhood assaulted him. *A spoon clanking on a tin plate. Iron bars that barred his view and prevented escape. Staccato footsteps on the floorboards and wicked laughter announcing his captor's approach.*

Damn. He'd seen what happened to captured boys who couldn't hold their own against a group of well-oiled cutthroats. He'd lived it. In fact, he'd been one of the few lucky enough to survive the docks in Bristol. But this girl wasn't Wolf. She faced brutal odds. These men were hardened by malcontent and misdeeds, and they punished first and asked questions later. Corsairs like these either turned boys into men or issued a slow and painful death to those who opposed them.

Violence certainly didn't favor the weak. Not in Saint-Malo, a citadel that bred pirates and privateers and some of the mightiest and most valiant sea dogs that ever sailed. Even so, the bloodthirsty claw-cat fought her captors. But she was in a precarious situation: if she revealed her identity, she could expect a crueler fate than the one she was suffering now. But if Wolf used her troublesome behavior to his advantage, he might be able to broker her release before she got her arse handed to her on a platter or found herself on her back servicing every last one of these scabrous dogs.

Corsairs didn't relax diplomatic practices for anyone, including female captives, unless it benefited them monetarily. They also had long memories. Malouines were willing to do anything for entertainment and profit, which meant he'd have to be a savvy barterer and offer them something they'd be hardpressed to get on their own—figuerados. The cigars originated from Portugal, and it just so happened that the entire region was steeped in war. He took his figuerado out of his mouth, stared at it, then growled, cursing his rotten luck.

His stare cut to the girl. Her wild desperation and courage was a rare find. Her curly hair was tied up in a handkerchief, her slender nose bloodied, and her mouth swollen. Her leather coat was too large for her frame and hung off her shoulders, the sleeves folded up at the ends to reveal clenched fists chained at the wrist.

Wolf's senses heightened, and he growled low in his throat. "What's going on here?" he asked a man to his right, barely controlling his temper. "What's this boy done?"

"Slave boy," the man spat. "Kicked that man there in the cock." He pointed rudely to two men. One limped, balls in hand, protesting loudly to the other who sat calmly at a table. "He won't be rutting for days, I wager." He arrowed his finger at another man. "And he sullied that one's grog. Been cowering in the corner like a rat ever since."

"Cowering?" Wolf scrutinized the girl's bloody knuckles. "I see a little rat baring its claws."

"Not right in the head, that one. He shouldn't bite the hand that feeds him."

"Depends on the hand." Wolf shook his head. Complete and utter fools, the lot of them. How long had the girl been held captive? Certainly not long enough to let her identity slip.

He clenched his fists, struggling to control the violent impulses coiling inside him. This wasn't England. He was a foreigner on French soil during a time of war. Losing his temper would only draw attention to himself, Joanna, and the girl.

He took a deep breath to curb his rising fury as another man goaded his captive into swiping at air. Dark circles discolored the skin beneath her eyes. Sod it, she looked as if she hadn't eaten a good meal in at least a fortnight, and she smelled as if she hadn't bathed in twice as long. He wasn't sure she'd even been given liberty to relieve herself.

"Thirsty?" a grizzled man asked her. He laughed and upended his tankard over her head. "This should cool you off."

"You . . ." She tried to hobble away, but with her chained ankles, she couldn't escape the ale that sloshed over her. She slipped on the floorboards and fell. "Oomph!"

"*Assez!*" A man missing several teeth broke away from the crowd and approached the girl as she struggled to stand. "Enough," he shouted again.

"*Diable!*" Regaining her footing, she glared at the man who'd bathed her in ale.

Her attacker turned his back. "You will learn not to steal my scraps, batârd, or you'll never eat again."

"Watch out, Cuvier!" someone shouted.

She wasted no time and leaped onto Cuvier, catching him by surprise, and pulled the chains dangling from her wrists taut around his throat. "You threw them to me!"

There was a distinct inflection in her voice that indicated French wasn't her native language. Bollocks. A foreigner, then. How far from home was she? She could be from anywhere in the world, but if she was from England . . . Hell, she might have been taught French as a member of the gentry or the peerage, which meant he couldn't possibly walk away now, even if he wanted to. It didn't matter that he had business of his own to attend to with Joanna or that he might finally receive the information he sought about his brother. Ignoring an Englishwoman's welfare simply wasn't the right thing to do. Hell, it wasn't his nature.

Cuvier tried to fling her off. When she wouldn't budge and his eyes started to bulge, he bit her hand.

She let go. He threw her down, gasping for air. "I'll watch you dance over hot coals for this!" he shouted.

Cuvier staggered, gasping for breath. Supported by his men, he lunged forward. Wolf stuck out his foot and sent the man sprawling into a group of card-playing gamblers, who'd been trying to ignore the ruckus.

"Watch what you are doing, *Diable blanc*!" a man shouted to an artful swindler who grabbed his earnings and leaped to his feet with unusual speed.

"*Mon Dieu!*" The devil raised his booty above the heads of the other men and then turned to glare at Wolf. "You owe me, *Monsieur*."

Men scrambled around the crafty sharker, but the gambler's attention never wavered from Wolf. His fiery stare promised there would come a time when he'd collect his due.

Get in line. Wolf glared back, unaffected. He puffed on his cigar and then shifted his attention to the girl.

As if sensing his eyes on her, the girl looked his way, locking her incredulous gaze with his. Wolf's breath caught as he found himself gazing into a pair of the stormiest gray eyes he'd ever beheld. Suddenly, the noise in the tavern quieted. His lungs squeezed, and alarm shot through him, the blood in his veins burning.

Dauntless, the little heathen didn't plan to back down. Like a bird fighting against the wind, she was determined to rebel against these pirates, including him, until she revealed her identity, or worse, breathed her last breath. Stubbornness would only get a person so far.

He understood her desperation to be free and the crazed flicker in her eyes. But that wasn't all he read there. A maddening intensity drove her, one he immediately identified with a mission, a search for something she'd never have a chance to accomplish unless she gained her freedom.

That wouldn't be easy, though. French corsairs were royalty in Saint-Malo. They'd been given the run of the place due to the many prizes seized by privateers and pirates in Napoleon's name, helping to fund the despot's quest for power and dominion.

Wolf removed the cigar from his mouth and slanted a glance at the well-dressed man seated among the others nearby. He wasn't anyone notable that Wolf could recall, but his clothing, comportment, and the way the men around him responded to his requests proved he wielded authority. As the other men threw scraps at the girl, taunting her, the leader chuckled, and Wolf had enough. Making up his mind to interfere, he plugged the cigar between his lips and crossed his arms over his chest to gain better access to the blades hidden within his wrist guards.

Cuvier wiped his nose as he lumbered across the floor toward the girl. "Beg for my forgiveness and I might show you mercy."

"Ha!" She thrust up her chained hands. "You don't have a merciful bone in your body."

Several men burst out laughing at Cuvier's expense.

"You're an animal," Cuvier said, "that needs to be caged."

"So you can strut about like you're my master?" she spat.

Wolf grew more impressed with her tenacity by the minute.

"Your *jailor*." Cuvier cackled. He clenched his fists, breathing heavily, and a look of retribution flickered in his eyes.

"*Combien*?" Wolf shouted, wanting to put an end to their sport. When he didn't get a response, he took his cigar out of his mouth and repeated his request more loudly. "How much?"

Cuvier spun around and spotted Wolf standing in the crowd. "This one is not for sale."

"Every man has a price," Wolf argued. He ignored Cuvier, choosing instead to address the disgruntled man enthroned at the table like an emperor surrounded by his devoted court.

Joanna rounded the bar and walked to the man's table, swinging her hips to and fro and garnering attention. She frowned at Wolf, then bent low and whispered something in the dictator's ear.

"Is that true?" he asked. At her nod, the man grinned and fixed his attention on Wolf. "Interested in that one, are you?"

"I'm shorthanded," Wolf admitted with a shrug.

Cuvier advanced. "You promised the boy would be our amusement, Robillard."

"As far as I can see," Robillard said, "he's become too difficult for you to manage."

"He's resourceful." Surviving what she'd been through while maintaining a disguise was a fete in and of itself. "A skill I can use on my ship."

Robillard nodded and then leaned forward, eyeing Wolf curiously. "Come, *Capitaine*. You and I both know this boy is not fit to sail. Why so interested in him, eh?"

"I happen to be in the market for a cabin boy." He took his time placing his cigar back in his mouth.

Chains rattled as the girl struggled against her captors and openly glowered at him. Alarm flickered in her eyes.

"This one? He's been nothing but trouble for us since the moment he was captured, *Capitaine*. I cannot recommend him to you."

"*Bon débarras!*" Joanna shouted with glee. "Sell and be rid of the mongrel, *mon amour*." She raised her hands, encouraging applause. The crowd responded, clapping and whistling, but Wolf understood Joanna's intention. She had a soft spot in her heart for children because her husband educated them in Dublin. And the sooner the girl no longer distracted Robillard and his men, the quicker Joanna could deliver her message to Wolf and he could disappear.

Joanna whispered something else in Robillard's ear.

"Is that so?" Robillard asked. He put his arm around the barmaid's waist. "You're a naughty wench, *ma chérie*. This boy will not be better off aboard the *Sea Wolf*." He considered Wolf thoughtfully. "You just told me its *capitaine* is a beast."

"Beast or no," Joanna said in character, smiling, "what do we care if he takes the boy, *mon chéri*? We will have more time to enjoy other pursuits, *oui*?"

Robillard considered her words for several tense moments before waving his hand in the air. "The boy is more trouble than he is worth. Cut him loose."

"But, sir," Cuvier argued. "We—"

"Silence!" The crowd hushed as Robillard bolted to his feet. "Do you dare to question my authority? I expect to be obeyed, Cuvier. My word is law."

Several men raised their fists and shouted in support of Robillard.

Wolf approached Cuvier. "Rest easy." He took a pull from his cigar and exhaled a cloud of smoke into Cuvier's face, making it momentarily fade from view. "I have ways of dealing with unruly boys."

"You will regret this," Cuvier said.

"Untie him," Wolf ordered, thinking the very same thing. But he couldn't allow her to continue to suffer, not when the girl reminded him of the boy he'd once been.

"We have not settled on a price, *Capitaine*," Robillard said calmly, raising his palm.

Joanna moved behind Robillard and slid her hands down his shoulders, molding her body enticingly to his. She whispered in his ear once more.

Robillard's response was instanenous. His eyes widened, and his head snapped up. "Do you make a habit of buying inexperienced boys?" he asked.

"That depends," Wolf said.

"On what, if I may be so bold, *Capitaine*?"

"On whether or not my current cabin boy has outlived his usefulness."

Laughter rose about them as Robillard's men caught Wolf's meaning.

"Aha!" Cuvier burst out laughing to boisterous applause. "Out of the kettle and into the fire, eh, boys?"

Robillard raised his hand again, halting their merriment. "So the rumors *are* true."

"Rumors have their purpose," Wolf said. "To frighten men and weaken opposition.

I will do almost anything to keep anyone from suffering the way I was forced to suffer.

"You avoid the answer, *Capitaine*."

"And you are wasting my time. Are you interested in getting rid of the boy or not?"

Robillard considered him carefully, and Joanna grinned. The tavern quieted, save for the sound of chairs scrapping against the floorboards as sailors, prostitutes, and gamblers waited expectantly for Robillard's next words.

Finally, he raised his hand. The nonverbal order set his men into action.

"Stay back." Her gaze frantically latched on to Wolf's. "Let me go," she pleaded.

Every muscle in his body primed for action as he watched the men roughly unlock her chains and then loosen them from her wrists and ankles. Her shackles noisily fell to the floor. She widened her stance and swayed on her bruised feet. She momentarily appeared vulnerable, folding in on herself as she rubbed the tender flesh left exposed on her slender ankles.

Robillard snapped his fingers. "So we are clear, *Capitaine*, I do not want to see this boy's face again."

The corsair's men shoved her to the ground in front of Wolf. He ignored his impulse to offer her a hand as she scrambled back to her feet. If he showed any measure of compassion, he'd alert Robillard and his men that this "boy" was not who he appeared to be.

Robillard's eyes lit up greedily. "Now let's talk price."

End of excerpt *The Mercenary Pirate* (The Heart of a Hero Series) by Katherine Bone

About the Author

A graduate of the University of Michigan with a major in history, Cora is the 2014 winner of the Royal Ascot contest for best unpublished Regency romance. She went on a twelve year expedition through the blackboard jungle as a high school math teacher before publishing *Save the Last Dance for Me*, the first book in the Maitland Maidens series.

When she's not walking Rotten Row at the fashionable hour or attending the entertainments of the Season, you might find her participating in Historical Novel Society and Romance Writers of America events, wading through her towering TBR pile, or eagerly awaiting the next Marvel movie release.

If you'd like to find out more about Cora or her books you can visit her online:

Website: http://coraleeauthor.wordpress.com

Newsletter: http://eepurl.com/bLwpm9

Facebook : http://www.facebook.com/AuthorCoraLee

Twitter: http://www.twitter.com/Cora_Lee49

Goodreads: http://www.goodreads.com/coralee49

Pinterest: http://www.pinterest.com/coralee49

Other Books By Cora Lee

Save the Last Dance for Me (Maitland Maidens, Book 1)

When Lady Honoria Maitland reunites with her old friend Benedict Grey, she proposes an arrangement: a faux courtship that will smooth wallflower Benedict's re-entry into society and appease her dying father. But Honoria's clever plan failed to account for Benedict's heart...or her own.

The Good, The Bad, And The Scandalous (The Heart of a Hero Book 7)

Andrew Elliott, Earl of Hartland, is no stranger to scandal. What the *ton* doesn't know is that Hart has received a warning: danger is heading for London and it's looking for Sarah Shipton. But marrying Hart throws Sarah from the frying pan of imminent poverty into the fire of a world filled with science and peril she never knew existed.